BOSS LOVE

BOSS #3

VICTORIA QUINN

CONTENTS

1. Hunt   1

2. Titan   15

3. Hunt   47

4. Titan   83

5. Hunt   137

6. Titan   171

7. Hunt   209

8. Titan   237

9. Hunt   261

10. Titan   277

11. Hunt   313

12. Titan   321

13. Hunt   327

Also by Victoria Quinn   333

Hartwick Publishing

Boss Love

1

HUNT

THE CITY LIGHTS bathed us in a gentle glow. Shadows were cast everywhere, the sound of our deep breathing filling the enormous penthouse. Her breath stuck to the window, even though she was sitting five feet away from it.

She was on her knees.

In front of me.

She obeyed without question, her face tilted toward the ground. Her slender back rose and fell with every breath she took. Even on the floor, she didn't look weak. She appeared strong, doing something she was so adamantly against.

For me.

My hands went to her shoulders, and I gripped their petiteness. My thumb brushed along her soft skin, watching the freckles disappear as I glided my thumb over the map of her body. My hands grabbed her long, dark hair and pushed it over her shoulder, bringing it down her chest and exposing her slender neck. My fingers glided across it, enjoying the milky white skin. I explored the nape of her neck even though I'd touched her hundreds of times. Now, everything was different.

This game was different.

I was so fucking hard.

I dropped my touch and stepped around her, watching her statuesque pose as I maneuvered around. My feet tapped against the hardwood floor, and my eyes never trailed away from her face. I watched her stare at the floor, never looking at me.

When I was in front of her, my body blocked the light and created a shadow over her face. I yanked my sweater over my head and tossed it on the floor beside us. She remained positioned in the same way, not giving the slightest hint of her discomfort. Her tits were firm and hard because she must be cold, sitting at my mercy like this. I undid my jeans and pulled them down with my boxers, revealing my reddened cock. More blood was circulating in my length than ever before. My head was so firm it could burst. I enjoyed letting her use me, but now that I was the one who got to do the using, I enjoyed it even more.

Her eyes moved to my dick in front of her.

I grabbed her chin and forced her gaze higher, commanding her to look at me. "Suck me off."

Instead of frustration in her eyes, there was only arousal. The look was subtle, but I'd seen it enough times from her to recognize it. She absorbed my commands without offense, letting me conquer her without stripping away her innate power. She pressed her face to my length and kissed it right in the center, her lips soft and wet.

"Yes, Boss Man."

She hesitated at my words, her back arching and her warm breath falling over my throbbing length.

"That's how you'll refer to me from now on."

She pressed another kiss to my length.

"Do you understand?" I grabbed the back of her hair and tilted her head back, forcing her to look up at me. I was already handling her much more aggressively than she handled me, but I couldn't stop myself. I felt like a powerful man for what I'd accomplished in my short lifetime. I was a wunderkind, someone who had risen to the top in the half the amount of time as everyone else. I didn't take no for an answer, and sometimes I got high off my strength. But I'd never felt more powerful than I did then—with Tatum Titan on her knees. Every muscle in my body tensed as I waited for her to yield to me, to bow to me with her words.

It was the first time she hesitated, the first time she struggled to do as I asked.

My cock hardened as I waited, my hand gripping the back of her neck. My dark eyes bored into her eyes, seeing the shimmering green color that was always in my dreams.

Her lips parted. "Yes...Boss Man."

My cock twitched. My breathing stopped. My hand tightened on her hair. A gentle sensation ruptured in my balls, the warning that a climax was fast approaching. I didn't shoot my load prematurely, but those few words would be enough to make me climax if I allowed my body to. I'd never heard anything so sexy in my entire life. There was no dirty talk I'd ever heard that compared to that.

I loosened my hold on her hair and guided her face to the base of my cock.

She did the rest. She started at my balls and sucked them into her mouth, using her tongue to massage them gently. Her saliva drenched the skin, making my balls wet and slick. She sucked another part into her mouth, devouring me like she did in my office so long ago. Then she moved up my base, dragging her tongue along the throbbing veins.

"Eyes on me."

Her gaze flicked up to mine as her tongue worshiped my dick. "Yes, Boss Man."

Jesus Christ.

She moved farther up my length until she reached the tip. She swiped her tongue across my head, licking up the lubrication I'd started to ooze. She sucked my tip gently, drawing out any extra that was hidden just under the surface.

It was worth it. Our arrangement was worth having this moment.

Having her.

She grabbed the base of my cock and lowered it to her mouth. She slowly drew her throat down my length, inserting him as far as he could go. She was a petite woman, and I had a big dick. We worked well together, but we couldn't overcome the impossible.

She looked up at me when she had a mouthful, saliva starting to pool at the corners of her mouth.

Damn.

She began to move, slowly pulling my cock out of her mouth before she reinserted him. She moved at a slow pace, probably understanding I was barely holding on. I wanted this to last as long as possible.

I bet she did too.

"Deeper."

She strained to shove more into her throat without gasping. She pushed hard, tears forming in the corners of her eyes. The saliva started to drip to the floor, drops forming on the hardwood floor.

Fuck, I wasn't going to last.

I wanted to come in the back of her throat, but I wanted to come deep inside her pussy. I wanted to start the initiation, to officially make her mine. This boss man had conquered his boss lady. I wanted every hole of her to be drenched with my come.

At least we had all night.

Before I allowed her to hit my trigger, I pulled my cock out of her mouth. It dripped with her moisture, glistening in the lights of Manhattan. My voice came out shaky despite my attempt to keep it stern. "On the bed."

She got to her feet then crawled on the bed, her ass in the air.

I grabbed her lace panties and pulled them down her legs, seeing her sex glisten the same way my cock was.

She definitely liked it.

I tossed her panties to the foot of the bed then turned her over, her back on the sheets and her head on the pillow. The mattress dipped as I crawled on top of her, her soft sheets greeting my palms. I covered her like the clouds covered the sun, blocking her from everything else. My arms hooked behind her knees, and I folded her perfectly underneath me, the right angle to fuck her deeply like I wanted.

I should put a towel under her ass because I was going to get come everywhere.

I held my shoulders above hers and looked her square in the eye, conquering her before I even shoved my dick inside. I could tie her up facedown and fuck her senseless, but I didn't want to. I could whip her with a crop, but I didn't want to do that either.

I had different plans tonight.

I guided the head of my cock to her entrance, and as if he knew exactly how to find it on his own, he slid inside her slick tightness. He dug deeper, stretching her wide apart, moving through her glistening arousal until I was sheathed to the hilt.

Her hands moved to my biceps, and she moaned.

I stayed buried inside her as I leaned down to kiss her.

Her lips failed to move with mine, overcome with the feeling of fullness between her legs. She moaned against my mouth, her breath shaky. When I kissed her harder, she finally responded to me. Her lips moved with mine, her tongue greeting mine with enthusiasm.

Our lips smacked as they glided together. When they pulled apart, I could hear the skin break. Our breathing was heightened in the quiet room, our arousal echoing off the four walls. The sheets rustled as we moved.

I started to thrust, getting myself deep inside her with every stroke. I invaded her pussy like an enemy conquering a hostile land. I claimed it as mine and intended to settle there for a long time. Her slickness sounded every time my cock slid through. She was soaking wet, my cock forcing the moisture to pool even more. I imagined it was dripping down her crack to the sheet beneath her.

Her hands slid up my shoulders until her fingers found my hair. She dug her fingers into it, feeling the soft strands as she twisted them. Her moans elevated, growing louder and stronger.

I knew what was coming. "You don't come until I say so."

All the light left her eyes as the command slapped her across the face. She actually looked pained, like my request was the most disappointing thing she'd ever heard.

"I'm gonna come inside you all night. And when I'm finished, I'll let you join me."

"Hunt, please—"

"Boss Man."

She hesitated before she corrected herself. "Boss Man..."

I slowly thrust inside her, giving her some sympathy by not fucking her hard like I wanted to. I rocked into her at a slow pace, letting my cock enjoy her soaking pussy. Sometimes I felt her walls tighten around me, the natural urge to come taking over. But then she righted herself again, stopping herself from feeling pleasure.

I wasn't sure how she still held on because I was about to slip away. Her cunt felt too incredible, her face too beautiful. Her tits were round and firm, her nipples pink and hard. My cock twitched as it remained buried inside her. I was ready to come, ready to explode.

And I didn't hold back.

I shoved myself as deep as I could go and came, my eyes locked on hers. A guttural moan escaped my lips, making me feel like a caveman who'd just completed his life's purpose. My eyes burned into hers, almost angrily. The head of my cock exploded as I dumped mounds and mounds inside her. I stuffed her good, making her so full that she started to drip from her entrance.

Her nails dug into my scalp, and she whimpered underneath me, a quiet plea escaping her lips. Forsaking her power was never a bigger regret than it was now. Now, she ached for her own release, to come around my dick just the way she used to.

This was payback.

I kept my softening dick inside her and started to kiss her, letting my mouth enjoy hers. My hand dug into her hair, and I felt my come drip out of her entrance as my length decreased. But it was only minutes before I was hard again, obsessed with this come-filled, wet pussy. I hardened back into steel again and started thrusting.

She dragged her nails down my back and began to writhe, her moans sounding like cries. She was frustrated, even angry with me. She wanted to come so badly.

But I wouldn't let her.

I thrust into her harder than I had the last time, pounding into her pussy and hitting her deep.

Her moans turned to screams.

I stared down at her as I positioned myself more squarely on top of her, bending her hips and angling her legs to either side of her head. The tip of my cock pushed through the swollen lips of her entrance, hitting the creamy channel, and then slamming into her cervix. I was determined to give her more come than last time.

"Boss Man...please." With fiery green eyes, she looked up at me with desperation. She wasn't above begging, even though pleading wasn't something Tatum Titan did. I was torturing her, and if she didn't find a release soon, she was going to lose her mind.

I was about to come again, and once I did, I would need a longer break. Since she'd obeyed me this long, I gave her some leeway. "Wait until I come..."

She grabbed my ass and pulled me more firmly into her. Now she fucked me harder than I fucked her. We crashed the headboard into the wall as we both sought to reach the finish line. She moaned as we moved, her sounds loud enough to break my eardrums. I was about to come, about to explode. I just needed a few more thrusts.

"God...I can't hold on any longer." Her face began to contort into that beautiful look she wore whenever she came. Her cheeks flushed pink, and her eyes widened as her plump lips parted, about to give way to a powerful scream.

I hit my trigger and moaned as I filled her, my cock dumping all of my seed inside her. "Come, baby."

She released the scream she'd been holding back, her channel tightening around my fat cock. Her come coated all over my dick, her white cream sheathing me from the hilt to underneath the head of my cock. Her hips bucked upward, and she dug her sharp nails hard into me, nearly scarring me. Her orgasm was a performance, and she should have walked away with an award for it.

I gave a few extra pumps even though I was finished, moving through the mixture of my come and hers. It was so warm and soft. Her cunt was made for my cock. I slowly pulled out of her and saw my come leaking from her pussy, sliding down her ass toward the sheets. I didn't hide my smile as I rolled over and lay on my back.

She took a few minutes to regroup, her eyes closed and her breathing deep and uneven. Slowly, she returned to a state of calm, recovering from the powerful explosion we both felt. When she was ready, she walked into the shower and rinsed off.

I put my boxers back on and set an alarm on my phone. I placed it on the nightstand before I got comfortable in bed, enjoying the luxurious sheets. There were soft and silky, and her pillow perfectly contorted to my head. I wasn't sure how Tatum Titan got up every morning when she had a bed like this. I ordered the best of everything for my homes, but she obviously had better taste.

Titan came back into the room fifteen minutes later, her hair still slightly damp but dried for the most part. She pulled on a t-shirt and panties before she sat on the edge of the bed. Not once had we turned on the lights, staying hidden in our mutual darkness. It set the tone for our new relationship, a change both of us could sense.

My arm rested underneath my head while the sheets were bunched at my waist. I closed my eyes, feeling my mind slip away as the cool sheets comforted me.

"Hunt?" Her voice sounded, but I wasn't sure how much time had passed since I'd drifted off before she said anything.

"Hmm?"

"You should get going before you get too tired."

I opened my eyes and stared at the ceiling. "I'm not going anywhere."

A tense pause filled the air between us. Like the end of a stick of dynamite, the rope caught flame and was slowly burning as it reached the base of the bomb. Her anger was mixed with potent alarm. "Excuse me?"

I sat up and grabbed her by the arm. I yanked her onto the bed, making her back hit the sheets. "I'm sleeping here. And you're sleeping beside me."

"I said I don't—"

I grabbed her neck and forced her gaze on me. "We're playing by my rules now, Titan." I positioned her beside me, spooning her from behind. My arm circled her waist, and I buried my face in the back of her neck. Her smell was mixed with mine, vanilla, and sex. I took a deep breath and let it out slowly, feeling more comfortable than I had in a long time.

Titan was as stiff as a piece of wood.

"Close your eyes." I didn't need to see her expression to know her eyes were wide open. "And go to sleep."

2

TITAN

THIS NEW REGIME WAS TERRIFYING.

Hunt had taken charge like he was born with this kind of power. He controlled me, forced me to do things I never considered before. I hadn't slept beside a man in nearly ten years—and now I did.

I barely slept that night, unable to doze off. Fear, panic, and anxiety consumed me most of the night. Those feelings weren't directed at Hunt, specifically. They were just emotions I couldn't control. Being unconscious would force me to let down all of my walls, but allowing that to happen went against my core.

So I only slept a few hours, on and off.

Hunt's alarm went off around six. He silenced his phone then stretched beside me, taking a few minutes to fully wake up. His large body shifted the bed underneath him, making the mattress dip slightly in the center.

I was the only person who slept in this bed, and now the mattress felt like a whole different place when there was a six-three man inside it. At two hundred pounds, he flooded the sheets with his innate warmth. He breathed quietly while he slept, the sound entering my silent bedroom. He shifted his position in his sleep. Sometimes, he grabbed me and pulled me closer, like I could slip away in his subconscious.

I lay still beside him, unsure what to do.

He turned over and pressed his body into mine. His hand moved up my shirt and cupped my bare tits, and he kissed my neck all the way to my ear. A quiet moan sounded in my ear as he felt me, his cock pressed against my back.

Despite my exhaustion, I felt the instant attraction.

He yanked my panties down and turned me until I was on my stomach. He crawled on top of me, his hips resting against my ass. Skipping the foreplay and getting right down to business, he shoved his enormous cock inside me with one single thrust.

Oh god.

He pressed his mouth against my ear and breathed as he fucked me, giving me a quickie that was solely about getting off. He didn't say a single word or make a single command. He fucked me in silence, our bodies slapping at every impact. Sometimes, he moaned right into my ear canal, and my pussy grew wet in no time.

I gripped the sheets underneath me and felt the chill up my spine. His cock felt so good inside me, his breathing sexy as hell. The scruff along his jaw brushed against my sensitive skin with every little move he made. I felt the orgasm start in my core and expand to all my extremities. A wave of pleasure shocked me, and I was pushed into a climax that made me bite the pillow beneath me.

When Hunt heard me scream, he pounded me harder, his pelvic bone thrusting against my ass. He dug his enormous cock inside me, pushing through my tight and wet channel and burying himself inside my slickness. He gave a long groan before he shoved himself completely inside and came, filling my body with his warm and heavy desire. He rested his face against the back of my head and breathed through the pleasure, his respirations slow and deep.

Having an orgasm first thing in the morning wasn't so bad.

He slowly pulled out of me, making sure his come stayed buried inside me. He got off the bed and walked into my bathroom. A second later, the shower came on, the water striking the tile on the floor.

I lay there for a full minute, recovering from the heat that was still burning between my legs. He hadn't said a single word to me before he fucked me exactly how he liked. He pressed his body on top of mine and fucked me in the laziest way possible, just wanting to come before he went to work.

It was sexy.

I still didn't like him sleeping here, but waking up to that was exhilarating.

When my body finally stopped pulsing, I joined him in the shower.

He obviously wasn't a morning person because he didn't say anything. He washed his hair and scrubbed his body with bar soap. He took turns standing under the warm water, allowing me to use it if I needed it.

I didn't say anything either.

A conversation didn't seem necessary. We were like any other couple in the world who had a morning routine with little talking. We were comfortable enough with one another that we didn't need to fill the silence with mediocre topics.

Hunt stepped out first and dried off before he moved to the bathroom sink.

And brushed his teeth with *my* toothbrush.

My fucking toothbrush.

Hunt looked at the reflection in the mirror, seeing my pissed-off gaze. Then he winked.

Jackass.

I got out and dried off before I dried my hair. Unlike in the evening when it didn't matter what I looked like, I had to take the time to style my hair perfectly, to curl the ends so they had a soft bounce. I did my makeup, smoky eyes with burgundy lipstick, and then pulled out one of the dresses Connor had given to me. It was a black with silver buttons along the top. It looked like a skirt and a blouse, but it was fitted into a dress instead. I slipped on the matching heels, added a necklace, and then I was ready to go.

I was Tatum Titan again.

I walked into the living room, unsure if Hunt would be gone by now. But he was in the kitchen, finished making a pot of coffee. He helped himself to the fridge and whipped up a quick breakfast of scrambled eggs and asparagus.

He made me a plate as well.

He sat down and enjoyed his breakfast while he went through the emails on his phone. His eyes narrowed every time he read something he didn't like, and he typed a quick response with his thick fingers.

I ate and tried not to stare.

He sipped his coffee slowly, careful not to spill

anything on his suit. He must have packed it in his bag, but it was a mystery to me how it wasn't wrinkled. Maybe he ironed it while I was doing my makeup.

We still didn't talk.

When Hunt finished his breakfast, he slid his phone into his pocket and set the plate in the sink. He came back to me, officially ready to go. He was clean and styled like he hadn't just spent the night with some woman. The only indication that his normal day was off was his beard.

I was surprised he didn't shave that with my razor.

"I'm making you dinner at my place. Be there at seven."

The breath rushed between my teeth, and I could barely swallow the command. Now I was at the mercy of this man, and his orders were law. I subjected him to this routine for six weeks, so of course, I had to uphold my end of the bargain.

But it didn't get any easier to swallow.

He stared at me, as if there was something I was forgetting.

I knew exactly what it was. "Yes, Boss Man." I looked away and sipped my coffee, no longer enjoying it.

He grabbed the back of my hair and yanked my head back so he could press a kiss to my lips. He ruined my lipstick before I even got the day started, but that didn't matter to either of us. He kissed me hard, giving me his tongue along with his aggression. It was like he hadn't just screwed me forty-five minutes ago.

He pulled away and walked to the elevator doors. "Have a good day."

"You too..." I was still blinded by that kiss, of being owned with just an embrace.

The doors opened, and he stepped inside. Before they shut, he said one more thing. "And pack a bag."

How's it going? Thorn's message popped up on my phone.

I knew what he was specifically asking about. *Not bad.*

But not good?

He slept over last night...

And how was that?

I didn't sleep, if that answers your question.

His playfulness seeped through the phone. *So, it went really well.*

I just couldn't sleep.

It'll get easier. You need to chill.

Thorn could never handle this situation, so it was bullshit for him to talk about it. *Maybe you need to chill.*

Nah. We both know you're the tight-ass in this relationship—and I like it. How about I take you to lunch?

I've got too much to do. But thank you. I didn't want to sit there for an hour and talk about being ordered to kneel. I didn't want to talk about my submissive life when it went against every fiber of my being.

I stopped talking to Thorn and focused on the tasks I had to finish by the afternoon. I had a few meetings lined up, and now that I was working with Hunt, I'd have to deal with him at some point during the day as well.

Lucky me.

Jessica spoke to me over the intercom. "Mr. Suede is here to see you."

He was? "Why?"

"He has a meeting with you this afternoon."

He does? "Are you sure?" I quickly pulled up my calendar and found the answer before she said anything.

"Yes. We booked it three weeks ago."

I juggled so many things that I couldn't keep everything straight. But I refused to admit my error to my assistant. "Send him in."

"Will do."

Connor walked inside minutes later, dressed in all black. He wore black jeans and a long-sleeve black shirt that fit his muscular body in the most flattering ways. It highlighted his impressive chest, his broad shoulders, and the intricate muscles of his arms. His dirty-blond hair looked great in contrast to the darkness, his blue eyes icy. "Titan." He walked up to my desk and extended his hand.

I walked around and took it. "Always nice to see you, Connor."

He gently pulled me into his chest and placed a kiss on my cheek—a long kiss.

Connor was great in bed. He knew how to fuck a woman long and right. The few times we'd hooked up, it was hot and fiery. But I'd never asked him to be anything more because he didn't fit the bill. And I didn't know if I could trust him to keep my secret. He was well-connected to every other industry on the planet. It didn't matter if they worked in tech or sports, everyone needed the right clothes to wear.

And Connor was a genius, frankly.

He looked down at my dress. "That's lovely on you."

"Everything you've made is lovely." I pulled away before the intimacy lingered longer than it should. If I saw a woman kiss Hunt like that, I wouldn't appreciate it. Even though my relationship with Hunt was temporary, I was committed to him. The kiss was harmless, but

I knew Connor still wanted me. I could feel it in the way he grabbed me.

"What can I do for you?" I moved around the desk again, putting the enormous piece of furniture in between us. I didn't blow off his advance, but I didn't welcome it either. Men didn't take rejection well, especially the successful ones.

He took a seat and rested his ankle on the opposite knee. This office was mine, but he invaded it with his presence. He was exceptionally confident, his presence projecting outward for a three-mile radius. Connor loved fashion, the statement fine clothes could make. It was considered a feminine art, but Connor was so masculine that it was abundantly clear he was straight as a board. He had relationships with his models, flings with his assistants, and one high-profile relationship that fizzled out after a year.

He was pretty and rugged at the same time.

The second he'd made a pass at me, I softened. I wanted those big hands all over my body, that hard mouth on mine. I took him back to my place, and he didn't leave until the following morning.

And we didn't sleep.

But now when I looked at Connor, I didn't feel anything at all. He was obviously attractive, still as self-assured as ever. He had a pristine reputation, the kind where everyone labeled him as a genius. He had everything I found attractive in a man—looks, wealth, and respect.

But now he didn't mean anything to me. He was just a face in the crowd, a few passionate nights that happened so long ago I could barely remember them. When I thought about sex, only one face sprung to mind.

Connor's hands came together on his lap, his fingers intertwining. He stared me down with the confidence of a man who wasn't scared of anything—not even me. "Are you seeing someone?"

The direct question caught me off guard. I thought Connor came here to talk about clothes, not who was between my legs. "Why do you ask?"

"I was disappointed when we didn't meet up after the fashion show. Then I wondered if you were already seeing someone. I didn't think to ask."

"You know I'm seeing Thorn."

His eyes narrowed. "I always got the impression that was a business relationship."

And he was dead on about it.

"I won't tell anyone my suspicions. That's safe between the two of us."

I didn't trust anyone—and he wasn't an exception. "I'm seeing Thorn. He and I agreed it was a smart business move for both of us. But over time...we've become very close." I wouldn't give Connor anything more than that. "I'm flatted by your interest."

Connor dropped it. "Very well."

I suspected that wasn't the only reason why he was there. He could have just called instead of taking time out of his busy life to meet me face-to-face.

"I'm here to talk about a sponsorship opportunity."

"Sponsorship?" Actresses and models were covered in a designer's clothing, representing their brand. But I wasn't an actress—and I certainly wasn't a model.

"The world is moving in a new direction, and I want to get on the ground floor. The number one consumers of my products are women. They want to be sexy, elegant, and classy. But they also want to be strong. So I'm launching a marketing campaign where I'm sponsoring the most successful women on the planet. I'd like you to be one of them."

"Again, I'm flattered."

"I have three names in mind, and you're at the top of my list. I'd like to shoot a few commercials and make a few ads. These images will represent power, female entrepreneurship. It'll be sleek, sexy, and strong." He held up his hands and started to frame the area around my cheeks. "The angles off your face and your eyes...will photograph so beautifully. I'm willing to make you a generous offer for your time. Since you're the richest woman in the world, I doubt that means a whole lot to you. I know you care more about image. And I think this will be a great way to capture your sophisticated beauty, to reach an audience of young women who aspire to be just like you. What do you say?"

The offer was generous. It allowed me to be a model, to wear gorgeous clothes and make a statement with them. Just like I did with the car, I was doing something in a new outlet. I already had a famous face, but now I was sculpting the world's perception of it. "Connor, I would love to."

A soft smile moved onto his lips. "That's wonderful." He rose to his feet and came around the desk to hug me. "I think this is going to be amazing." He pulled me into his chest, his strong arms tight against my lower back. "I can't wait to see your face in my ads. You'll take Suede to a new level."

"I hope so," I said. "But honestly, I'm just doing it for the clothes."

He chuckled as he leaned back to look down into my face. "You and everyone else."

THORN CALLED ME WHEN I GOT HOME FROM THE OFFICE.

"Hey, I talked to my mom today."

"Oh?"

"Want us to stay with them for a few days. I have to be in town for work anyway. You're free next weekend?"

I didn't have anything pressing on my schedule. "I think so."

"Great. Mom will be excited."

"Guess what happened to me today?" I walked into my penthouse and immediately slipped off my heels. They were beautiful, but they hurt like hell.

"You bought another business?"

"No. Connor Suede stopped by and asked me to be in a few ads for him. He's going for a strong, feministic look. Wants me and a few other successful entrepreneurs to be part of it."

"Wow, that's really cool. First the Bullet and now this."

"I think it could be good marketing, a way to get the world to see successful women in a way that isn't sexist."

"We're already heading in that direction. This could help."

"Plus, I get to keep the clothes."

He chuckled. "Of course, that's important to you."

"If Connor asked you to model for him, you'd want to keep the goods too."

"True. Hopefully, he asks us to do a husband and wife fashion line."

"Maybe." Hunt's face suddenly appeared in my mind, but I had no idea why.

"You wanna do something tonight? I feel like I haven't seen you in a while."

It was the second time he'd asked me to do something in a single day. Now I worried something was wrong. "I already have plans with Hunt. Everything alright?"

"Yeah, everything's good," he said quickly. He sounded truthful, his voice deep and playful like always. "Lunch tomorrow?"

"Yeah. I'll pencil you in."

"See you then." He hung up.

THE DOORS OPENED, AND I STEPPED INSIDE HUNT'S penthouse. The colors of his living space were all brown and black, distinctly masculine and dark. His couches were made of leather, and he had two cigars sitting on his coffee table. I considered announcing my presence, but I suspected he already knew I was there.

He stepped out of the kitchen, the sleeves to his long-sleeved shirt rolled up to his elbows. He was in dark jeans, and his jaw was shaved. His brown eyes greeted me warmly. "Hey, baby." His arms circled my waist, and his hands rested in the small of my back. He kissed me softly, greeting me like a man would greet his wife.

It was nice.

His gentle kiss turned sensual when his tongue moved into my mouth. He made an innocent kiss sexy without really trying, bringing it to a new level of hotness. His hands slid to my hips, and he squeezed them before he stepped back. "Hope you're hungry."

For sex, not food. "Yeah."

He set the table, putting an Old Fashioned on the table.

I sat down, surprised he wanted to eat instead of skipping to the good stuff. I took a drink and enjoyed the taste, knowing he could make a good drink.

He sat across from me and ate his salmon. "How was your day?"

"Good. Yours?"

"Good." He kept his eyes on me as he ate, watching me like I was a TV screen rather than a person.

"What?"

"What?" he repeated back to me.

"You're staring."

"I can stare all I like." He took another bite of his

food, his gaze unwavering. He'd made salmon with greens. "If you can't handle this, wait until we're finished with dinner."

He was even more aggressive than he was when I first met him. I was talking to Hunt, one of the most powerful men in the city. When he had the upper hand, he wasn't afraid to use his strength.

I'd be lying if I said I didn't like it.

"Where's your bag?" he asked.

"My what?"

"Your bag," he repeated, his gaze ice-cold. He didn't take another bite of his food, holding his fork tightly in his clenched fingers. "The one I told you to bring."

I didn't leave it behind to be disobedient. I genuinely forgot. "It slipped my mind..."

"Nothing slips your mind." His eyes were as dark as coals.

"I don't do sleepovers. So yes, I did forget."

"All of that is about to change. You should get used to it." He finished his food first then stared at me as I finished mine.

I refused to be intimidated by his fierce gaze, so I ate at a normal pace, taking my time and not rushing just because he was finished. "This is good."

Silence.

"You made it?"

"Yes."

"I thought you weren't a good cook."

"My skills are limited, but the things I do know how to make, I make well." His gaze didn't lighten in intensity. He looked at me like he could barely restrain himself from grabbing me.

"If all you want to do is screw, you didn't have to bother with dinner."

It was the first time his gaze broke, when he didn't seem so aggressive. "I realize that. I wanted to cook for you."

I faltered before I took another bite.

"Most of the time, all I want to do is fuck you. But I enjoy your company just as much."

I felt the same way. Hunt had slowly become my friend. When he was possessive and aggressive, it was hard to remember that, but a kind soul still existed behind those cold eyes. I finished my final bites of food, wiping the plate clean.

Hunt stood up the second I was done, his chiseled forearms covered with veins that looked like rivers. He took my plate but left my drink behind, knowing I would want it. "Go into my bedroom and strip down to your panties. Now."

He was issuing the orders like a commander in the armed forces. He took to the position well, immediately molding to it like our relationship had been this way the entire time. He was a good leader, pleasing me while he pleased himself. But I would always struggle to agree, always struggle to follow orders. "Yes, Boss Man."

I downed the rest of my drink and walked into his bedroom. It was exactly the same as I remembered it, a gray duvet-covered bed with black dressers and end tables. He had a white rug on the floor and a painting of an indistinct image on the wall. Piece by piece, I stripped off my clothes until I was in just my panties.

I didn't know where to wait, so I sat on the edge of the bed and crossed my legs. Minutes passed before he finally joined me. He walked inside in only his jeans, which hung low on his hips. He was barefoot and bare-chested. With short hair and aggressive eyes, he looked absolutely delectable.

For a second, I didn't care that he was the one in charge.

He looked so perfect, his abdominals endless lines of hard muscles. He didn't possess an inch of fat, his body a mass of bones and muscle. He was sinewy and strong, thick in the thighs and lean in the legs.

He leaned against the doorframe as he looked at me, examining my bare tits. I automatically sucked in my belly, not wanting him to see it hang out. When he stared at me like that, I couldn't help but stare at him in the same desirable way.

He stepped into the room and approached the bed, his muscular arms looking cut as he came closer. His hands went underneath my ass, and he gripped my lacy panties. Slowly, he lowered them down my thighs.

I uncrossed my legs and lay back, lifting my hips so he could get them down my long legs. He pulled them to my ankles before he tossed them aside. He pressed my feet against his chest and ran his hands up my legs, feeling the smoothness of my soft skin. He turned one leg and kissed the inside of my knee. He did the same to the other.

My thighs tensed, as did the area between my legs. My breaths turned to pants, and I ached to pull his jeans off. I wanted that gorgeous body on top of mine, so I could kiss him as he kissed me.

He set my legs down then moved to his jeans. He took his time taking them off, the zipper sounding loud to my ears. He pushed them past his thin hips then dug his fingers into the waistband. Slowly, he tugged them down his body and past his knees. His fat cock popped out, already drooling at the tip.

Now I didn't care about sleeping over.

He pulled me to the edge of the bed, my ass hanging over just a bit. Then he pointed his length across my sex, slowly grinding back and forth. Moisture pooled at my entrance, coating with him with the shiny residue. He tilted his hips slightly and slipped inside my soaked channel, sliding all the way to my back wall.

I closed my eyes and moaned, feeling more like a woman when I was full like this. He was the only man who made me feel this incredible, who made me feel this good. My hands went to his wrists, and his hands gripped my hips. I planted my feet against his chest, his pecs like two slabs of concrete.

He moved inside gently, thrusting until his body rubbed against my clit. Then he pulled out again, treating this like a marathon rather than a sprint. He brought his fingers to his lips and sucked them.

I stared at his actions, unsure what he intended to do with those fingers.

He removed them from his mouth then pressed them to my back entrance. He gently pulled at the back, pushing through my tight flesh.

I'd never done ass play before. I'd never been into it, and I'd never had a partner who told me they liked it. Since Hunt was the one calling the shots, there was nothing I could do about it anyway. I stayed relaxed, feeling his enormous cock push into me over and over. When his fingers were deep inside me and he stretched me, it felt good. My nerve endings fired off everywhere and heightened my overall experience.

I should have known Hunt was an ass man.

He wrapped his arm around my thighs and kept me positioned as he thrust and fingered me. He was in control like he'd done this hundreds of times. He'd probably had women beg him to fuck them in the ass—two at a time. He'd done everything in the book, explored every possibility. This was nothing to him.

That would explain why he was so good in bed.

His hips rocked over and over, pushing his cock deeper inside me.

I was about to come. My hands reached for him, needing to hold on to his powerful body. I wanted to grip his forearms, his biceps, anything.

"No."

I growled in frustration, knowing exactly what that word was in answer to. "Hunt..."

"Don't make me ask you again."

"Boss Man," I corrected.

"The wait won't be much longer." He pulled his fingers out of me just as he removed his cock. He was coated in my moisture, slathered in my arousal. He kept my feet glued to his chest as he leaned over farther and pushed his head into the back hole.

The one where his fingers had been.

I gripped his hips and steadied him, stopping him going in.

He looked down at me, aggression heavy in his gaze. "Ever been fucked in the ass, baby?"

It was a personal question, but since it was about to happen, I told the truth. "No..."

"I'll go easy on you." He slowly pushed inside me, his head having a difficult time getting through the entrance. If this were my pussy, he would push his way through with a violent thrust. But he slowly sank into me, going easy just like he promised.

I breathed through the strain, tensed as I felt my body stretch in ways it'd never been stretched before. His large size hurt. I'd be lying if I said it didn't. He was already big for my pussy.

He was enormous for my ass.

He slid farther until most of his cock was buried inside me.

I breathed harder, taking in the pain without wincing.

Hunt pressed his hands on either side of me on the bed and looked down at me. "You okay, baby?" The man I knew had come back to me, not the controlling dictator I'd unleashed. He was thoughtful and compassionate, caring about making me feel good, not about hurting me.

It reminded me that I trusted him.

"Yeah, I'm okay."

He grabbed the backs of my thighs and pinned my knees against my torso, forcing my legs apart and away from my chest. He started to thrust, using slow and even strokes.

It hurt.

But it felt good at the same time.

I held on to his wrists and dug my nails into his skin, doing my best not to cut him. I breathed in with every thrust and released the air from my lungs when he pulled away. I had an enormous cock in my ass, so no matter how gentle he was, it was going to hurt.

Once I got used to it, he started to move harder. His eyes remained glued to my face, his jaw tightening in pleasure. His enjoyment was obvious, impossible to hide. He wanted to fuck me just like this for a long time.

I felt the tears prickle in my eyes, bubble at the corners, and slowly drip down my cheeks. I wasn't crying, but my eyes smarted naturally. I felt so many things at once, so many full sensations.

"Want me to stop?"

When I gave him twenty lashes, he never asked me to stop. When I asked him to get on his knees, he didn't walk away. He did everything that I asked, even when my requests were difficult to fulfill.

I couldn't give up.

I couldn't walk away.

"Fuck me harder."

His eyes darkened with shadows, and he shoved himself completely inside, sheathing every inch of his huge cock.

My nails cut into his skin then, leaving dents where every single finger had been. I let out a gasp, but that was better than the scream I was holding back.

He thrust into me hard, rocking the bed and screwing me just as he would if his cock were in my pussy. He grunted and panted with the movements, on the verge of exploding deep inside me. He obviously couldn't hold on any longer because he pressed his thumb against my clit and rubbed it aggressively. "Come, baby."

The size of his length was painful. His thrusts made it even worse. But there was something so sexy about it, the release of powerful endorphins as my body was put through so much. There was so much pleasure with the pain, so much to be enjoyed despite the discomfort.

He rubbed me harder, his breathing deep and ragged as he restrained himself. His eyes roamed over my body, enjoying my curves as my tits shook with the thrusts. After a few more pumps, more touches, I was there.

I came.

And I came hard.

"God..." I squeezed his arms so tight I must have bruised him. My head rolled back, and I let out a scream that could shatter the windows. My body had been elevated to a place above the stars. The experience was surreal, taking me to the heavens and beyond. I felt a million things at once, saw more than I could absorb.

It was more powerful than any other orgasm I'd ever had. Hunt gave me something I didn't even know I was missing.

Hunt grunted as he released, filling my ass with all of his come. He shoved himself completely inside me, pressing his forehead to mine. He pumped me with his desire, had done something no other man had done before. He took me in a new way, giving me an experience I'd never considered having.

He stayed inside me even when he was finished, his breaths in tune with mine. His cock slowly softened, and I felt the pressure decrease throughout my body. Every time he took a breath, his smooth cheek pressed against my tits. He had me pinned and folded underneath him, a man taking a woman so carnally it was animalistic.

He slowly pulled out of me, and my body winced as it readjusted to his absence. He pulled out then stood upright, a muscular man covered in sweat. He eyed his handiwork between my legs, seeing the come as it started to drip out. That usual look of arrogance came over his face, like he had just conquered a land and laid waste everyone who didn't surrender.

All the power was taken from my hands, leaving my helpless and completely submissive. It went against my nature, the backbone of who I was. I didn't put up with anyone's shit, and like hell would I allow my man to order me around. But when Hunt was the one in charge, I enjoyed the game. I enjoyed fulfilling his fantasies just as he had fulfilled mine.

He turned his back on me and walked into the bathroom. A moment later, the shower came on.

Now that my body relaxed and I caught my breath, I was eager to wash off.

Although, I wasn't eager to sleep.

I HELPED MYSELF TO ONE OF HIS T-SHIRTS I FOUND IN THE drawer. He didn't have a hair-dryer, so I had to do my best with the towel. The strands were damp, but after a few minutes of hitting the air, they would be back to dry.

Hunt sat up in bed, his tablet in front of him. He was shirtless, his powerful physique appearing chiseled by the light from his lamp. His fingers dragged across the screen as he read through something.

If I were home right now, I'd probably be working or drinking. That's what I usually did in my spare time. I pulled back the sheets and got into bed beside him, still feeling strange sharing a bed with another person. I was exhausted because I hadn't slept the night before. I'd try to sleep tonight, but I suspected it would be another struggle. He couldn't expect me to stay with him every single night for the next six weeks.

That was unrealistic.

I got comfortable in bed and tilted my head toward the window, watching the never-ending commotion of the city. Just a few blocks down, I could see my building.

Hunt set his tablet aside then slid across the bed toward me. He lay beside me, his body pivoted into mine. His heavy arm circled my waist, and he rested his chin on my shoulder. With every little touch, his coarse hair scraped against my soft skin. The smell of body soap and his natural masculine scent came over me, surrounding me in a bubble. His sheets already smelled like him, and everything about his bedroom reflected his stern personality. His thick thighs grazed mine underneath the sheets. "You doing okay?"

"Yeah." Even if I weren't, I'd never admit it.

"Because you can tell me. I'm not going to think less of you."

Silence.

He kissed my shoulder. "I know I have a big dick, baby. One of my flaws."

That made me release a sarcastic chuckle. "I'm sure it's lost you a lot of dates…"

"You'd be surprised."

"No woman ever turned down a guy because his dick was too big."

"All women are made differently…some smaller than others."

"Well, I'm pretty small, and I take it just fine."

"But you have an iron pussy." He chuckled against my shoulder. "It's indestructible."

I felt his hand move to mine on my stomach. His large fingers interlocked with mine. He closed his eyes.

I didn't close mine. "Why do you want me to sleep with you?"

His opened again at the question. "Because that's what people do after sex. They screw then sleep."

"Not true. And that didn't answer my question."

He was quiet, as if he wasn't going to answer my question at all. "Maybe I actually like you, Titan."

"Nobody likes me," I whispered. "I'm ruthless and controlling."

"And you're also smart, funny, and sexy—in addition to being ruthless and controlling."

"That still doesn't make me a great teddy bear."

"I disagree," he said. "Why are you so repulsed by the idea of sleeping with me?"

"It has nothing to do with you, personally."

"Then what's the reason?" he pressed.

I could never tell. "I just don't like it. If a man made the same statement, no one would question him for it."

"Not true."

"Yes, true."

"How did you sleep last night?" he asked.

"I barely slept at all."

He propped himself on his elbow and looked down at me. "I don't snore, so why is that?"

"I've been sleeping alone for a long time. I'm not used to sharing a bed."

His eyes studied my lips like he'd find more answers that way. "You can fuck me for six weeks, but sleeping beside me is still weird to you?"

"It's nothing personal, Hunt."

"It is personal," he whispered. "I thought we were friends."

"We are."

"Friends trust each other. And I can tell you don't trust me."

"That's not true."

"It is." He lay back down and looked at the ceiling. "Which is a shame, because I trust you." He reached over and switched off the lamp at his bedside. The bedroom was immersed in darkness, and he turned away.

I felt guilty when I shouldn't. Hunt meant more to me than all the others. I saw him as someone who could be a lifelong friend, someone I cared about. I obviously wasn't showing those feelings very well. I wasn't good at being emotional, at wearing my heart on my sleeve.

I moved to his side of the bed and pressed my body against his back. Now I was the one who spooned him, my tits against his shoulder blades and my face against the back of his neck. "I do trust you, Hunt. You're one of the people I trust most, actually..."

The only reaction he gave was his simple breathing. His back rose and fell with every breath, and he didn't move an inch. He just lay there, pretending I didn't exist.

I wasn't getting anything out of him.

Then he spoke. "Prove it, Titan."

3

HUNT

I LIKED RULING OVER HER.

I got what I wanted, when I wanted it.

But she obeyed with hesitance, remained reluctant when she shouldn't. I shouldn't expect anything else, but I was disappointed anyway. She told me she didn't sleep with anyone, whatever her reasons might be. But I expected her to feel differently with me.

I wasn't sure why.

Women had always wanted me because I had money, fame, and fancy cars. They wanted to fuck me so they could brag about it to their friends. They wanted to party with me so the paparazzi could snap a picture of them and put it on the cover of a magazine. They never wanted me to leave, and if they got to sleep in my bed beside me, they wouldn't want to leave me either.

Titan was the first woman who wasn't impressed by me.

She was like a robot. The only time she showed passion was when we were screwing. She finally came alive and showed real emotions. The rest of the time, she was just as cold as she was during meetings. Only once in a great while did she let her walls down and show that soft smile that grew from her heart.

I was impressed with Titan.

But I was more obsessed with Tatum.

Who was she?

I woke up to the sound of my alarm the next morning. Titan was awake beside me, but it wasn't clear if she had already been awake. I rolled on top of her, gave her a quick morning fuck, and then got into the shower.

She helped herself to my bathroom, using my toothbrush just the way I used hers. She caught my reflection in the bathroom mirror and winked.

That put a smile on my face.

When I finished getting ready for the day, she put back on the clothes she'd been wearing and slipped on her heels. If she'd brought her bag like she was supposed to, she could have left for work right away.

"I'll see you later." She rose on her tiptoes and kissed me before she walked into the elevator.

I stared at her ass when she faced the other way, thinking about the way I fucked it last night.

She turned around, a knowing look in her eyes. She probably knew exactly what I was thinking. Titan had a knack for that sort of thing. The elevator doors shut, and she was gone.

I went to work and handled a few phone calls. The entire building was buzzing with activity. There was so much to do and so little time. Even if I worked constantly around the clock, I still wouldn't be happy with my productivity.

Pine called me before ten.

I answered. "Surprised you're awake."

"Why?"

"It's not noon yet."

"Shut up, asshole." He insulted me, but he laughed at the same time, making it easy to question the validity of his sincerity. "I got a special invite to that new club that's opening downtown. And you and Mike are coming with me."

"When?"

"Tonight."

"It's Wednesday."

"So?" he asked incredulously. "When have we not partied in the middle of the week? Every day is a good day to party when you are hot shit like us."

I only had six weeks with Titan, and I wasn't going to squander it by pretending to hook up with someone. If Titan would just drop her uptight paranoia, I could bring her along or at least explain why I wasn't interested. "I'm gonna pass, man."

"What?" he snapped. "Why?"

"I'm meeting with the Megaland guys."

"At nine?" he asked incredulously.

"I don't know when the meeting is going to end."

"Get real," he snapped. "Mike and I are coming to get you whether you like it or not." He hung up on me.

That little bitch hung up on me.

I WENT TO THE NEW BUILDING I OWNED WITH TITAN. IT was a few blocks away from my main building, so my driver drove me there and dropped me off. A lot of people recognized my car, so if I didn't want to draw attention to myself, I took the shiny black Mercedes with tinted windows.

I rode the elevator to the top floor and walked into the conference room. Our offices were still under construction.

Titan sat at the head of the table—drinking an Old Fashioned.

At ten in the morning.

Since she could handle her liquor pretty damn well, I wasn't going to judge her for it. "I've been thinking about the new name for the company."

"Let's hear it." She straightened in her chair and turned her full focus on me.

I sat in the chair on her right with the windows in front of me. No one else was on this floor because the rest of it was being remodeled. Titan and I liked our privacy until we could find appropriate assistants who didn't have any loyalty to Bruce. "Stratosphere."

Her eyebrows rose, and a smile full of approval formed on her painted lips. "I like it."

"It's perfect."

"I think so too. We're in agreement." She took out her notebook and wrote the word in her slanted, feminine writing. "I'll contact our lawyer and get the corporation going."

"Sounds good."

Titan went over a few other things that we both needed to address. Anytime she presented information to me, everything was so meticulous. She chased down any loose threads, needing to know every little detail about everything. She didn't leave anything to chance.

She was a great business partner. If I was going to have anyone in my corner, it was her. She also had a well-honed intuition, reading people so well it was like she was looking at their private file.

"I scheduled a meeting with a new supplier," she said. "They're overseas, and they're half the cost."

"How?" Slave labor?

"They use a type of material that's much cheaper to make. They have surplus over there, but it's in demand over here."

I could get on board with that. "Great."

"I also cut a lot of costs here." She pushed the paper toward me. "If Bruce paid more attention to what he was doing, he could have saved this company."

"Well, he was an idiot."

She pushed another paper toward me. "This is the stock value. It spiked last week."

I eyed it, surprised by the sudden growth. We had barely done anything, so I didn't understand why the value had increased.

"I think it's from that commercial we did with Brett," she said. "People are investing in us as the new owners, not the products."

That made sense. "That worked out well."

"I'm also starting a new campaign with Connor Suede. He wants to do a series of ads and commercials with the most powerful women in the world. I think that will only help."

My eyes darted to her face at the mention of his name. I saw the text message that popped on her phone weeks ago. I saw the way he spoke to her, leaning in like he was about to kiss her. She wasn't the only one with intuition. If he hadn't fucked her already, he obviously wanted to. "No." The word flew out of my mouth all on its own. I didn't think twice before I laid down the law.

Titan slowly turned to me, her eyebrow arched. "No what?"

"You aren't doing that commercial. Connor Suede is a prick."

"Do you know him?"

Hadn't met him once. "Doesn't matter."

"No, it does matter. He's the biggest fashion designer in the world. I wear his clothes almost every day."

It was the first time I wanted to rip the clothes off her body and not because I wanted to fuck her.

"It would be great PR for us."

"We don't need PR." I pushed the stock reports back toward her. "We're good."

She pushed it back. "Hunt, what is your problem?"

There wasn't room for jealousy in our relationship. We didn't even have a relationship, just an arrangement. But something carnal inside me flared up, made me angry. My jaw was clenched, and the veins in my fore-arms were strained. "Did you sleep with him?"

Titan used to compose her features at all times, but now she let her real emotions come out. Her features softened in surprise before they hardened once again in offense. "Excuse me?"

"You heard what I said." The question was on the table, and I couldn't backpedal. I had to see this through. I needed to know what kind of relationship they had if they were going to work together.

"That's none of your business, Hunt."

"I fucked you in the ass last night. Yes, it is my business."

She looked like she was about to stab me with her pen.

Every time I tried to calm myself down, I just got worked up again. Red in my gaze and I couldn't see straight. I was calm, logical, and pragmatic. But the idea of another man touching Titan made me anything but cool. I guess I was the jealous type.

Never knew that before.

"Hunt, you're playing with fire right now." She pressed her finger to the table, drawing an invisible line between us. "Back off, or you're going to get burned."

"Then burn me," I said coldly. "I'm the one in charge for the next six weeks. You're going to tell me exactly what I want to know. Now."

Her eyes narrowed. "That's not how it works, Hunt. I never pried into your personal life."

"Well, you should have."

"I respect your privacy."

"I don't want you to respect it, and I sure as hell don't respect yours."

She sat back, floored by what I said.

"I'm tired of pretending that this is just some convenient fuck-a-thon. We've both made sacrifices for each other. We're in business together, a first for each of us. You know more about me than most people, and I know more about you than you usually tell. We aren't friends. We aren't lovers. We're something else entirely. So all those rules you set up don't apply to us. So, tell me, Titan. Did you fuck Connor Suede?"

She held my expression as she stared me down, her eyes shifting back and forth slightly. She erected a fortress of stone and brick, impenetrable. But no matter how thick her fortifications were, I could break through every single one. She might be made of stone, but I was made of bullets. I could pierce right through her.

"I don't know what this is, and I'm not going to put a label on it. But it's not what it started as. It's grown into something different, an exception. So let's just be honest with each other. That's one rule that still applies."

She pressed her lips together tightly, her expression hardening. "Yes."

"Yes, what?"

"I fucked Connor Suede."

I already suspected her answer, but hearing it didn't make it easier to swallow. It was like a big pill without water. My hand rested on the table, and my fingertips tapped against the surface. Instead of letting my anger out like a monster, I kept it buried inside—for the most part. "When?"

"A while ago."

"What does that mean?" I kept my voice steady even though it was easier said than done.

"About six months ago. I don't see why the time is relevant since it never overlapped with you."

"I'm just wondering why he's still trying to fuck you."

Her eyes remained as cold as two pieces of green ice. "You've been with me. I'm sure you can figure it out…"

Because she was an unforgettable fuck. I knew it, and she knew it. I tapped my fingers against the table.

"Do you feel better now?" she asked sarcastically. "Or did that not change anything at all?"

"Why did you sleep with him?"

"Why?" Both of her eyebrows leapt high on her forehead. "Because he's handsome, confident, successful… Do I really need to explain how sexual attraction works?

Why don't you tell me about the last woman you slept with, and then justify why you did it?"

It was a stupid conversation. She proved her point.

"You know what, Diesel?"

I'd never heard her use my first name before. It wasn't in an affectionate tone, but in the way my mother used to say it when I did something wrong.

"I liked you the moment I met you because you weren't a prick like all the others. I've always felt like an equal with you, respected and validated in the same way as the rest of your colleagues. You've never scrutinized my decisions because I'm in a skirt instead of pants. Men like you are what we need in this world. In order for women to be granted the same respect as their male counterparts, men need to treat us equally. You've already done that, setting the stage for others. But this...this is a double standard. If I were a man, you would not ask me why I slept with Connor. You're judging me for something your friends Pine or Mike would have done." She leaned forward and held up her hand. "I'm not going to put up with it, Hunt. I'm not going to be vilified for being a sexual human being exercising my right to do whatever the fuck I want to do." She slammed her hand on the table, the sound thudding in the conference room. She leaned back in her chair and crossed her arms over her chest, staring me down like scum on the bottom of her shoe.

She made me feel like shit when I'd never meant to offend her. "Before you start hating me, let me explain…"

"Explain what?" She was back to being cold and objective, like her speech had never happened.

"I didn't ask you about Connor because I'm judging you…or think less of you for having meaningless sex. I think a single woman can do whatever she wants. The number of partners she's had is irrelevant. Just like how the number of partners I've had doesn't matter. That's not what I was implying."

"Seemed that way."

"I was asking because…it's obvious, Titan."

She cocked her head to the side. "What's obvious?"

"It's obvious that I'm jealous." I confessed my crime, knowing I had no right to feel that way.

Her features slowly softened.

"I admit," I said quietly, "when I saw Connor touch you at the fashion show, I didn't like it. When I saw him text you and ask to come over…I almost broke my jaw from clenching my teeth so hard. I don't have anything against the guy…but I hate anyone who's ever had the pleasure of enjoying you. As far as I'm concerned, you're my woman. I'm possessive. I'm jealous. I'm selfish." I looked out the window when I didn't want to be the recipient of her gaze anymore.

Now there was just silence.

A lot of it.

Instead of working, we soaked up the tension. It was supposed to be an afternoon of deadlines and plotting. But somehow, our sexual relationship was at the forefront of the conversation.

I'd already thrown myself under the bus, so there wasn't anything left to say. I explained my behavior, telling her she meant more to me than she should.

"Hunt..." She pursed her lips again, taking her time deciding what to say.

I already knew what she would say.

"If I'm being honest, I'm jealous too."

Okay...that was not what I was expecting her to say.

"When we were at the fashion show, some model was pressed up against you. I felt the acid flood my mouth, but I stopped myself from giving in to the jealousy. I stopped myself from caring. But I did care..."

Tatum Titan was jealous. Couldn't believe it.

"So, I do understand."

My natural reaction was to smile, to feel the victory spread through my limbs. But I kept my reaction under wraps. I steadied myself from doing something to shatter her vulnerability.

"I like you a lot, Hunt."

This was getting better.

"Sometimes it scares me," she whispered. "It's so rare for me to find someone that I trust, to find someone I feel so connected to. In the past decade, I've only made a handful of genuine friends. When I met you...I wasn't expecting to make another. I've felt comfortable with you since the beginning, that you respected me for my brains and my talent, not just the way my legs looked under my skirt."

"But you do have nice legs..."

She looked at me, a small smile growing on her lips.

I smiled back. These were the moments I lived for with Tatum. I loved getting to know the woman underneath those executive clothes, that hard face. She was as soft as a rose petal, silky to the touch.

"The sex is great for a lot of reasons. But I think one of the biggest reasons is this feeling between us...camaraderie, friendship, trust...whatever it is. I've never partnered with anyone before, and when I considered doing it with you, there wasn't a doubt in my mind. That tells me there's something here."

My smile slowly faded away as my heart rate picked up.

She looked away for a moment, staring at her silver pen on the desk. "But what I said in the beginning still applies. I'm not looking for romance. I'm not looking for love. I'm just looking for an arrangement that gives me pleasure. And when it's over...we'll walk away but stay friends."

It was like someone shot me in the chest.

Right in the heart.

Blood poured from the wound, and I struggled to breathe.

With every beat, I was losing my life.

Sometimes, it seemed like I meant something to her, but at the end of the day, I didn't.

Why should I care?

"Why aren't you looking for love? Why is that off the table?"

Her eyes turned back to me. "I'm marrying Thorn. I can't fall in love with someone."

"Are you implying you could fall in love with me if you let yourself?" It was a bold question to ask, but since we were being honest, I decided to go for it. I didn't have anything to lose.

She searched my expression as she considered the question, taking her time. "I...I don't know."

Tatum Titan had just hesitated and avoided eye contact.

"That sounds like a yes to me."

She turned back to me, hardening her gaze once

again. "When you're sleeping with someone, emotions get complicated. I just have to remind myself what I want...and not let things get messy. I've never allowed anyone to control me. Giving you that luxury automatically tells me you mean something different to me."

"And the fact that I've let you control me tells me the same thing."

A long pause.

Intense eye contact.

Noticeable heat in the room.

It was like a furnace was burning a forest.

My eyes didn't drop from hers. I stared her down, refusing to look away.

She did the same time, her green eyes resembling emerald flames.

She was the first one to break the silence. "Then that means we need to be careful...because we both want different things."

"You still want to marry Thorn?"

"I committed to him."

I leaned forward in my chair, coming closer to her. "You didn't answer my question."

"Yes, I did."

"I asked if you *wanted* to marry him, not if you were committed to doing it."

"Aren't they the same thing?"

I shook my head slightly. "Not at all."

Titan broke eye contact for a second time. "I think it's the best move."

"Your love life doesn't have to be a business decision."

"My entire life needs to be a business decision. I can't make another mistake."

Another? "You've made a mistake before?"

Her gaze met mine once again. "Yes, as we all have."

It was her ex-boyfriend. I could feel it. "It's okay to make mistakes, baby. They humble us. They strengthen us. They turn us into a powerful people like Tatum Titan and Diesel Hunt. Mistakes make successes mean something. And I sure as hell have learned far more from my mistakes than I have from my successes."

She watched me, her eyes submissive.

I rested my fingertips against my chin, brushing across my coarse hair. My eyes remained on hers. "I think we could have something pretty incredible if we allowed ourselves to." I put my cards on the table, gambling my chips away.

She stilled at the statement. "Are you saying you want something with me?"

I shrugged. "I'm open to it. Are you?" I kept my hard expression, but I was holding my breath at the same time.

"I've made a commitment to Thorn. He's a good man, and I'll be happy with him."

"And bored."

Her eyes flashed with annoyance. "Love like ours is the kind that lasts. He's powerful, trustworthy, everything I'm looking for. And even if he wasn't, it's been done."

"You haven't signed a marriage license."

"But I don't break my promises."

Thorn made her promise to marry him? What kind of man would do that? A proposal shouldn't be coerced. It should be wanted.

"And Hunt, you have the rest of the women in New York City to bed. A man such as yourself wasn't built for a single woman."

"I don't know about that." I rubbed my fingertips against my lips. "I'm enjoying having you."

"For now." She turned away and grabbed her papers. She cleared her throat, silently dismissing the conversation. "I'm doing that campaign with Connor. We'll start shooting in a few days. I'm running late to lunch. I'm meeting Thorn."

I didn't want her to meet Thorn either. I was jealous of the man who'd secured her so long ago. I was jealous of how committed she was to him, how she deemed him to be the only man good enough to share her life with.

I rose out of my chair the moment she did. "I'm coming over at seven."

She looked up at me, her hair pulled over one shoulder. She accepted my statement without argument. "Yes, Boss Man."

Before she could walk away, I circled my arms around her waist and pulled her in for a kiss. I kissed her hard on the mouth, my hand digging into her hair. My fingers grazed along the soft skin of her neck, gliding over her pulse and to the fall of her hair. I kissed her with passion, angst. I kissed her like she was the only woman in the world I ever wanted to kiss.

And she kissed me back.

The kiss lasted for minutes. She obviously didn't care about being a few minutes late if it was for a good reason.

And this was definitely a good reason.

When I finished, I pulled away with my hand still on the back of her neck. "Thorn Cutler will never kiss you like that." My fingers released her reluctantly, but my eyes bored into her in a way they never had before.

I WAS JUST ABOUT TO WALK OUT THE DOOR WHEN I CAME face-to-face with Pine.

"Going somewhere?" He waggled both of his eyebrows.

"You're stalking me now?"

"I have to because you keep blowing me off."

"I'm not blowing you off. I'm busy, man."

"Well, you're busy a lot lately. You've never had a hard time squeezing in a party here and there."

"I told you I'm meeting the Megaland guys tonight."

"It's seven o' clock. Bullshit."

"Work never sleeps. You know that."

"Shut up and let's go. I'm not leaving until you come out with me." He blocked the door with his body.

"You think that's gonna stop me?"

He shrugged. "Probably not. But I'll just follow you if you don't come along. And we both know you don't want me to follow you...because you're hiding something."

I was hiding something.

"Maybe you're fucking a princess from Thailand or the press secretary at the White House, I don't know. But you can fuck her later. Let's go."

Pine had me cornered, and his suspicions were right on the money. But at least he didn't suspect Titan was the woman I was screwing. That was one thing to be thankful for.

NIGHTLIFE WAS THE SAME EVEN THOUGH I'D BEEN OUT OF the game for a while. It was a bunch of neon lights, darkness, waitresses in tight skirts, and tits.

So many tits.

Two girls made out in front of me, trying to seduce me so I'd take them back to my penthouse. Their tongues moved in tandem before they sealed their mouths together. They groped each other's tits through their dresses.

I watched them as I drank my Old Fashioned, knowing it was the only way to keep up the pretense that I was single and fucked anything that moved. Stuff like this usually turned me on. I liked girl-on-girl action as much as the next guy.

But I didn't feel anything right now.

There was one place I wanted to be—with Titan.

The sex with her was hotter than any threesome I'd ever had. I wouldn't want to watch her make out with another woman. The only thing I'd like to watch is a recording of me fucking her.

Pine had a girl on his arm, some black-haired woman with almond-shaped eyes. Mike was making out with a blonde. The music constantly thudded against my ears, the sound blaring and loud. It was going to give me a headache by the end of the night.

"Quite the show." Brett came out of nowhere and fell into the seat beside me, his eyes on the two women making out in the chair beside me. "Admission is free, right?"

"Not for you."

He chuckled and kept watching them. "Wow. I don't even kiss that well."

"Female intuition."

Brett watched them as he rubbed the side of his face. He hardly blinked.

My phone vibrated in my pocket. I pulled it out and saw a message from Titan. *Since it's been two hours, I assume you aren't coming.*

I'd meant to give her a heads-up, but I never had a chance. *Got caught up. I'll be there around midnight.*

Well, maybe I won't be.

She was pissed. But I liked it when she was pissed. She was mad I wasn't there, which meant she wished I were there. And that was excellent news to me. I smiled before I shoved my phone back into my pocket.

"Seeing anyone?" Brett suddenly asked.

I nodded to the two women. "Right now, them."

Brett stared at me. But it was an unusual stare.

Heated, intense, intimidating...he'd never looked at me that way before.

"Everything alright?"

He drank from his glass, his throat shifting as he downed the liquid.

I kept staring at him, waiting for some kind of explanation.

"Be straight with me, man."

"Sorry?" I raised an eyebrow, unsure if I was reading his expression correctly. It was dark and he looked mad, but I wasn't sure if he was truly mad. What the hell would he be mad about?

"I asked if you were seeing someone."

"And I said no."

"Which is a lie."

My ears stopped vibrating with the bass of the music, and now my heartbeat was heavy in my ears. I could hear it as well as feel it. My brother never had a problem calling me out on my shit, and he was doing it now. And he was always right before he started a brawl.

He knew about Titan.

How? I didn't know.

Why did he decide to mention it then? I didn't have a clue. Fortunately, my friends seemed caught up with their dates, so they didn't care about me. The music was too loud to overhear us.

Brett looked just as angry as he had a minute ago. "Why are you lying to me?"

I still didn't have a confirmation that he was referring to Titan, but I suspected he was. "How did you know?" I baited him into it, seeing what he would say.

"The way you talk about her. You kiss the ground that woman walks on."

"Do not," I snapped. "I just respect her, admire her."

"And that text conversation you just had."

Was I naïve to assume my brother wouldn't invade my privacy like that? "That was a dick thing to do."

"I didn't look on purpose. The screen is bright as fuck, and her name was right at the top."

"That doesn't mean anything. We work together."

His eyes narrowed. "You're gonna lie again?"

My brother had me. There was no getting out of it. I didn't say anything to incriminate myself further.

"How long has this been going on?"

I'd promised Titan I wouldn't tell anyone, and now I felt like I'd betrayed her. But in my defense, I didn't tell him anything. And I wouldn't tell him about our arrangement. That was something I could protect, at least. "A few months."

"What about Thorn?"

How did I get around this one? "They've...kinda got an open relationship."

"So, she's not cheating?"

"No," I said quickly. "Titan would never do that."

Now that I was talking to Brett, he seemed to ease up. "Why are you keeping this a secret?"

"She doesn't want anyone to know. I would have told you, but...she told me not to." I nodded to Pine and Mike. "They don't know either."

"Is that supposed to make me feel better?" he asked incredulously. "I'm your brother."

"It's not like we talk about women anyway."

"We do if we're seeing them for a few months."

It wasn't how it seemed, but I couldn't correct him. "I don't think it's gonna last. Another reason why I didn't want to mention it."

"Why not? You're running a company with her now."

"She's just not...looking for anything serious." I turned back to the women making out on the couch. "And it's not like I am either. I just enjoy being with her."

Brett stared at the side of my face.

"Keep this between us, alright?" I said. "I mean it."

"You can trust me, Hunt. You know that."

"Yeah...I do."

"So, you guys are just fuck buddies, then?"

I nodded. "Pretty much."

"You're a lucky man, Hunt." He shook his head in

disbelief. "Not too many men are man enough for a woman like that."

I certainly was.

"But she seems like a really cool person. If it were me...I'd have a hard time not falling for her."

I stared at the girls harder, brushing off what he'd said.

Brett let it hang in the air, probably on purpose.

I hoped this conversation was finally finished. The longer it continued, the more likely someone could catch on.

"Why don't you take off and go to her?" he asked. "You'd obviously rather be there instead of here." He nodded at my friends. "And they won't even notice you're gone."

"And ditch you?"

"Ditch me?" he asked incredulously. He turned to the two women with their hands up each other's dresses. "I'm taking these women home tonight. Don't you worry about me. Now go home to the woman you've been thinking about all night. If I were you, that's where I'd be."

THE ELEVATORS DOORS OPENED AT MIDNIGHT. I WALKED

into her penthouse and found her sitting on the couch. I didn't pack my bag because I came straight to her place. I'd have to wake up early so I could head back to my penthouse and get ready before heading to the office.

She was sitting on the couch, a glass of red wine in front of her.

That was a surprising change.

She greeted me with a simple look. "Ran out of whiskey."

I smiled as I moved toward her. "Now it makes sense." I moved to the spot beside her on the couch and immediately dug my hand into her hair. My hips wanted to thrust inside her, and I wanted to give this woman enough come that it dripped down her thighs when she stood in the shower. Fortunately, she was in just a t-shirt, so I pulled it up past her hips.

She pressed her hand against my chest, immediately pushing me off her. "You had fun tonight, huh?" With a tone full of furious accusation, she didn't look as aroused to see me as I was to see her.

"Not really."

"Didn't seem like it."

I moved my body forward again, guiding her back to the couch. "Were you there?"

"No. But someone with a camera was."

I grabbed her panties and started to pull them off.

She slapped my hand away, her eyes full of daggers. "Looked like you had a threesome."

"Someone took a picture of me watching those chicks make out?"

"Yeah...you seemed pretty into it."

"I'd rather watch you touch yourself."

She slapped me across the face, her palm smacking hard against my skin.

I turned with the hit and felt a scorching surge of arousal. I slowly turned back to her, turned on and pissed off. "I wouldn't have been watching two women get it on if I could just tell my friends that I'm seeing you. But you don't give me that luxury." Since she was already furious, I didn't want to add fuel to the fire by mentioning Brett knew about the two of us.

"You could have not gone."

"Pine came by my place. I told him I had to work, but he didn't believe me. I've been blowing him off for weeks. I don't blame him for being annoyed. But if I could tell him the situation, he would knock it off."

"Not gonna happen."

After our conversation that morning, she still couldn't trust me? "You really are uptight."

Smack.

I wasn't planning on her slapping me, but I liked it.

After I turned with the hit, I looked down at her. "And you have a tight ass."

She slapped me for a third time.

This time, I yanked on her panties hard, ripping them slightly at the seams. I quickly got my slacks and boxers off, forgetting about the shoes and crawling on top of her. I pinned her down, hooked one leg over the back of the couch, and slid inside her.

So fucking wet.

I paused as I was seated inside her, feeling the warm tightness surround my length. I had been staring at those two women when I could have been doing this the entire time. Seemed like a waste. "Now I know why you're so mad. You've been wanting me to fuck you all night." I started to move inside her, using slow and even strokes.

"God, you're cocky." She bit her bottom lip as she unbuttoned my shirt, getting it open so there was nothing but skin between us.

"Yes, I'm a cocky god." I buried her into the couch and moved between her legs, being greeted by more moisture as I got the momentum going. I thrust hard and deep, causing her ass to leave a print on the cushion.

She enjoyed me so much that she didn't give me shit about the arrogant comment I'd just made. She grabbed on to my hips and moved with me the best she could, taking in my long length with eagerness. "Hunt...yes."

"Tell me you missed me."

She looked me in the eye as she dug her nails into my chest. "I missed you..."

"More."

"I missed you, Boss Man."

I thrust harder, all the muscles in my back firing off as I fucked this woman good. I gripped the back of her neck as an anchor, keeping her in position so I could fuck her as deep as I wanted. "Fuck yes."

She moaned as she fucked me back just as hard. We'd done kinky things together, but we'd never fucked quite as hard as this. We were doing whatever we could to feel each other, to feel that shattering sensation of euphoria.

"Ask my permission to come."

For just a second, her eyes lit up in rebuttal. But it quickly melted away when her desire to climax outweighed her pride. "Let me come, Boss Man."

"Beg." I deepened the angle and thrust deeper, our mouths together and my tongue in her mouth.

"Please..."

"Please what?"

"Please, Boss Man...let me come."

I gripped her hair harder and forced her gaze

directly into mine. "You were jealous tonight. Admit it."

She breathed into my mouth, her nails dragging down my back.

"Tell me."

"Yes...I was jealous."

"Jealous of what?"

She moaned as I fucked her harder, barely stopping herself from coming. "Of you watching them..."

"And?"

"I want you to only watch me."

Now I wanted to come. I wanted to fill her with all my seed and watch it drip everywhere. That sentence was the sexiest thing I'd ever heard her say. "You can come, baby..."

Right on cue, she exploded, her pussy clenching my dick with everything it had. "Boss Man...yes...god." She pressed her face into my neck, cut me with her nails, and writhed with me, sweat streaking across her body.

I gave two more pumps before I exploded inside her, dumping all of my arousal into her cunt. That was what I'd wanted to do all night, not watch some women try to fulfill my desires. I already a woman who knew exactly how to do that.

She laid her head back, breathing hard and with pointy nipples.

"Say thank you." I commanded her with my eyes,

forcing her to obey.

She almost didn't. She struggled with it, struggled more than when I asked her anything else.

I grabbed her hair and yanked on it. "I just fucked you the way you liked. Now thank me for it."

Her eyes were sizzling pans, and a single drop of water would make them spit with steam. A woman like her didn't need to thank any man for fucking her, but I wasn't any man. I was the man who owned this woman until our arrangement was finished. She had to say it if she wanted me to keep fucking her. "Thank you..."

The muscles of my ass and back tightened in reaction. I got the most powerful woman in the world to thank me for making her come, making her legs shake in a powerful climax. I owned every inch of her, and she knew it. This power, this strength, was something that sent me all the way to the moon.

Now I was hard again.

I started to thrust. "Good. Now I'll make you come again."

IT WAS TWO IN THE MORNING WHEN WE GOT INTO BED. I slept in the nude because I was too tired to pull my boxers on. Thankfully, my alarm on my phone was automatic, so I didn't need to worry about setting it every night. I often didn't know where I would end up at night, so it was one less thing for me to worry about.

Titan got into bed beside me, her face washed and ready for sleep. She pulled on my collared shirt, the one I'd been wearing out at the bar. It smelled like booze, sweat, and cologne.

"You're going to sleep in that?"

"I prefer your t-shirts, but this will do."

"I can always leave a few over here..." I smiled when I pictured her having an attachment to my clothes. She could afford to buy the most expensive shirts in the world, the most comfortable, but she chose mine.

It had nothing to do with the fabric.

"No," she said. "That's okay." She lay beside me and pulled up the sheets. But she was stiff, not relaxed like she had been with me that morning. Anytime we were in this bed together and we weren't having sex, she was rigid like a board. She stared at the ceiling blankly, counting down the hours until morning finally returned.

I thought this objection would end after the first or second night, but she obviously wouldn't let it go.

"Would this help?" I stayed on my side of the bed, a foot of space between us.

"What?" she whispered, slowly turning her head

toward me.

"If I stayed here all night. Didn't touch you."

"If you want to be helpful, you could just go."

"No. You need to get over this. You're never going to sleep with Thorn?"

"I'm sure we'll have our own bedrooms."

"And your kids won't think that's odd?"

She shrugged. "It'll be one of our weird hang-ups."

"It's a really weird hang-up," I said honestly. "You're a fearless woman who isn't scared of anything. Don't you think it's time to overcome this? You're being a pussy right now, Titan."

Her eyes snapped open in disbelief. "Did you just call me a pussy?"

"Yep. And I meant it."

Her eyes narrowed. "You shouldn't talk about things you don't understand."

"Then educate me. You said you would be willing to tell me."

"I said I was willing to consider it."

"Well, you've had plenty of time."

"Two days..."

"That's enough time. Now tell me."

She looked at the ceiling again, her answer obvious.

This woman was such a pain in the ass. "Back to what I was saying. What if I stayed over here?"

"I don't know."

"And I promised not to touch you. It's like not I'm not even here. You know, baby steps."

"I guess we could try it. I haven't slept much in three days. I'm exhausted."

What kind of fear would possess her to stay awake for nearly three nights straight? "Alright. You have my word. I won't touch you."

"Really?"

"My word is pretty damn powerful."

She extended her hand to me.

I eyed it, having no idea what she was doing.

"Let's shake on it."

I couldn't suppress the chuckle in my throat. "Fine, if that works for you." I shook her hand then stuck to my side of the bed.

She adjusted her pillow, tossed and turned a few times to get comfortable, and then fell asleep immediately.

I could tell by her breathing.

I didn't sleep right away. Instead, I watched her sleep beside me, her eyes closed and her lips slightly parted. Her hair was across the pillow, and my collared shirt was loose around her body. When Titan was at her most vulnerable, she was also the most beautiful.

I wished I could see this version of her every day.

4

TITAN

WHEN MY ALARM went off the next morning, I realized I'd been asleep that entire time.

And I could actually think clearly.

I turned off the alarm and looked at Hunt beside me. He was on his side of the bed, one arm tucked under his head while the other held up his phone. He scrolled through his messages. He seemed to have been awake for the past few minutes.

"Sleep well?" he asked with a husky voice.

"Actually...yeah."

"I kept my promise."

I wiped the sleep from my eyes and finally felt energy in my body again. Crunching numbers and plotting my business empire was nearly impossible when I couldn't think of two coherent sentences in a row. Now my mind was fresh again. I could enjoy the beautiful view outside my window for the first time in days. "Thank you."

"Baby steps." He kicked the covers back, revealing his throbbing cock against his body. Long and thick, his nine inches were impressive every time I looked. "So." He propped himself up on his elbow and looked at me. "Can I cross the line now?" He straightened his fingers and drew a line down the center of the bed.

"Yes."

"Good." He circled his arm around my waist and pulled me to the center. He moved on top of me and separated my thighs with his own. He moved between my legs and pushed his thick cock inside me, sliding until he was completely sheathed. "I love dumping my come inside you first thing in the morning." He got right down to business, stimulating my clit with his pelvic bone and shoving his cock deep inside me. He thrust hard and fast, pushing me into a quick orgasm followed by his own. When he finished, he pulled out of me and immediately got into the shower.

As I sat there with his come lingering inside me, I had to admit I liked morning sex too. There was no kissing or introductions. It was straight sex, right to the point. It was quick and good, skipping the foreplay because neither one of us needed it.

It was a great way to start the day.

My driver was taking me to Stratosphere.

Thorn called me. "What's up, Titan?"

"You called me." I scrolled through the emails on my tablet.

"That's right," he said. "Wanted to know if we could use your plane this weekend."

"What's wrong with yours?"

"Yours is newer," he said. "Also, mine is in maintenance."

"Sure, that's fine."

"Great. How's it going with your boy toy?"

"Pretty good actually." The divider was up between my driver and me so he couldn't overhear what I was saying.

"And the sleepovers?"

"Gotten better."

"Really?" he asked in surprise. "You actually slept?"

"Yeah. He promised he wouldn't touch me in the middle of the night. I know he's a man of his word, so I was able to sleep."

"Wow. Talk about progress."

"Yeah."

"Hmm."

"What?" I asked.

"Nothing," he said quickly. "You two just seem to be getting close."

"I think we've always been close. I see him every day."

"But close in a different kind of way."

"How so?"

"I don't know... I didn't see you getting over the sleepovers."

"I wouldn't say I'm over them," I said. "I just found last night tolerable." My driver pulled up to the building, so I had to wrap up the call. "I've got to go. I'll see you tomorrow."

"Alright. See ya."

I hung up and walked into the building. I took the elevator to the top floor and stepped out into the open room. The conference room door was closed, so I assumed Hunt was already inside. I made a cup of coffee before I stepped in. "Hey."

"Hey." He eyed the Styrofoam cup like it was an oddity.

"What?"

"What are you drinking?"

"Coffee."

Now he was in shock. "You drink things other than booze?"

I rolled my eyes and sat down. "Shut up."

When he chuckled, he wore the sexiest smile. It was charming and endearing, revealing the sweet version of this man that very few people got to witness. His navy tie matched his suit, which was the same deep royal color. He was looked good in every suit he had, but this was a particularly good color on him.

"You look nice today," I said bluntly.

He adjusted his tie. "Thanks. You don't look too bad yourself."

I opened my folder and got to work. We spent the next two and half hours focusing on everything we needed to get done. Hunt was right to the point when it came to business, skipping over things that didn't have the same priority. He could compartmentalize tasks, never forgetting the least important stuff, but shelving it for a later time. He was quick with his reasoning, overruling me in a lot of things because he had a better approach. He'd done business in this space a lot longer than I had, so he had vital expertise to share.

He was a great partner.

"I'll make sure this is all wrapped up by tomorrow afternoon," he said. "Because there will be no work this weekend." He gave me that intense expression I'd come to decipher immediately. Its meaning was as plain as a sunny day.

He wasn't going to be happy with my news. "I'll be in Chicago this weekend."

"Why?" He didn't raise his voice or change his tone, but he somehow brought more authority into the words.

"Thorn and I are visiting his parents. They're hosting an event for their company."

Hunt's expression didn't change, but he somehow looked ruthless. His dark eyebrows came closer together, and his coffee-colored eyes no longer looked warm like a fall morning. He looked dangerous, like coal sitting in the bottom of a mine. "You aren't going."

This exchange of power was becoming more difficult to bear. We interpreted authority in different ways. I only commanded him to come to me, not forbade him from going other places. His sense of control extended far and wide, taking the meaning in a much different way. "That's an abuse of power."

"There are no safe words with us. So there are no rules."

"I already told them I'm going."

"Then tell them you aren't going."

"Hunt—"

"You aren't carrying on with Thorn on my time, Titan. I own you for the next six weeks."

"I never told you where to go and not to go."

"But you didn't care what I was doing when you

summoned me. I'll summon you just the way you did to me—and you better come on your hands and knees."

I respected his fire but also despised it. "I'm stuck, Hunt. There's nothing I can do. His parents planned this months ago—"

"Not my problem."

I steadied myself from rolling my eyes. "Well, I'm going. There's nothing you can do to stop me."

"Except handcuff you to my bed." He cocked his head to the side, making the threat more real.

"Then I'll leave you when you least expect it."

"You're that determined to defy me?"

"I'm that determined to keep my word to Thorn. I've been blowing him off enough as it is."

"Like I haven't been blowing off all my friends," he said coldly. "At least he knows about me."

I couldn't argue with a man who always had the upper hand. "I'll be back Sunday night. It'll only be two evenings."

"That's too long. But if you insist on going, that's fine."

I couldn't believe he caved that easily after all the things he'd said. "Really?"

"Because I'm coming with you."

Now that was a twist. "What?"

"You'll stay with me at my hotel. Go out and do your

thing. But the second it's over, you're coming back to me."

"We usually stay with his parents..."

"Then I'm staying with them too, or you're staying in a hotel. Your pick."

I didn't doubt that he'd make good on his word. "You really want to go all the way to Chicago for the weekend?"

"I really want to stuff you with come before you go out with your in-laws."

I felt dirty for actually being turned on by that. "Then we'll stay in a hotel. I guess that's the only compromise we're going to find..."

"Works for me."

I didn't know whether it was his jealousy or his possessiveness that was taking over. But either way, his mood had darkened, and he wasn't as easygoing as he had been minutes ago. He wanted to have me every second of his six weeks. He wanted me to be his prey, his plaything.

It was one time I actually didn't mind it.

MY GOWN ARRIVED RIGHT TO MY DOOR, AND I TOOK IT IN the plastic wrap and hung it up in the living room so I wouldn't forget it on the way out tomorrow. It was deep teal, tight against every inch of my body, and soft. I had a white-gold bracelet to wear with it, and the straps hung off my shoulders to reveal my collarbone.

It was beautiful.

It was one of the few things that I didn't get from Suede.

The elevator doors lit up again before they opened.

Did the delivery man forget something?

Hunt appeared in dark jeans and a long-sleeved olive-green shirt. His hands were in his pockets as he stepped inside, his entire body hard and defined all over the place. He welcomed himself inside and didn't say a word.

We'd have to start being more careful about him stopping by all the time. If anyone with a camera noticed how often he came to my building, it would take a minimal amount of research to figure out he didn't live there—but I did.

He eyed the dress I'd just hung up and the shoe box on the couch. He came closer to me, his presence filling my massive penthouse. His jaw was recently shaven, not a spot of hair on his chin because he shaved after work.

He stopped directly in front of me, his face just inches from mine. He looked down at me, eyeing my lips and then my eyes.

I held my breath, feeling a surge of sensations. My fingers prickled, my pulse quickened, my hair stood on end, my pussy moistened. Everything happened within the snap of a finger. I was heavy in lust, so deep in carnal desire that I was lost in a heavy fog. Everything else was blurred out, and the only thing I could see clearly was Hunt.

This beautiful man.

His hand slowly slid up my arm, to my shoulder, and then up my neck. He never broke eye contact with me as his fingers reached the fall of my hair. He gently wrapped my strands around his fingers, forming a knot between his hand and my hair. He stepped closer to me, his presence so near our bodies blended together.

I just breathed.

I didn't know what overcame me, but I felt weak. All my strength and desire disappeared. I just wanted this man to take me, to make me feel incredible. I wanted him to kiss me all over, to suck my nipples until they were raw.

He pressed his forehead to mine. "I missed you."

Goose bumps flooded my arms as the words sank into me. I felt the shiver all the way down my spine to the backs of my heels. We did amazing work together. We had very different minds, but we both brought significant contributions to the table. But when we weren't discussing ideas, our sexual chemistry perfectly complemented one another. "I missed you too."

He kissed the corner of my mouth, his lips lingering there for a long time. His fingers brushed against the back of my neck, making me shiver. "I know you did." He dragged his mouth against my bottom lip playfully, enticing me. "Undress and get in bed." His fingers slowly snaked out of my hair. "Wait for me."

His request was clear, and I found it easier to obey than I had before. Now that I wanted him so much, I was eager to have him in any way I could. "Yes, Boss Man..." I walked into the bedroom and stripped all my clothes away. The lights were off because I never bothered turning them on. The view of the city always brought a powerful glow into my bedroom, making everything visible without a single light turned on. He didn't tell me what position to take, so I got on all fours with my ass in the air, assuming that was how he wanted me.

It was usually the position all men preferred.

I heard the sound of glasses moving and liquid pouring. He was obviously helping himself to a drink, making me wait on purpose.

Asshole.

The TV turned on, and I imagined him sitting on the couch taking his time.

Bigger asshole.

All I could think was about that mouth on my body, that enormous cock making me feel so full, the way his breath fell on my neck as he rocked into me. He wore the sexiest expression when he looked at me, a dark visage accompanied by a hard jaw. I felt like the only woman in the world when he thrust into me, burying his enormous length inside me.

Time dragged on forever.

He was making me wait on purpose, making my pussy glisten for him in anticipation. My back arched on its own, and I waited for the sound of the TV to turn off.

No man had ever made me wait like this.

I finally heard the TV turn off and his footsteps tap against the hardwood floor. He was already barefoot, and I imagined his shirt was lying over the back of the couch. His masculine presence entered the bedroom and approached the bed, his thick arms resting by his sides. His torso was a combination of hard lines and grooves, a man etched from stone. He stopped at the foot of the bed and stared at me.

I stared at the headboard, waiting for him to do something.

I heard the sound of his belt hit the floor. Then he pulled his boxers down his muscular thighs and kicked them aside.

My back arched harder.

"You really miss me now."

"Yes..."

His body shuffled as he got to his knees on the hardwood floor. He pressed his face between my legs, greeting my swollen lips with his own. Very faint stubble from his jaw grazed against my inner thighs as his mouth worked my entrance.

"Oh..." I gripped the sheets underneath me and closed my eyes.

His tongue circled my clit before it delved inside my pussy. He tasted me, feasting on me. His big hands gripped both of my cheeks and squeezed. His large mouth licked and sucked all of me, becoming more aggressive.

My arms weakened, and I could barely hold myself up anymore. My head dipped toward the bed, and I breathed hard. My hand reached behind me, and I found his wrist, needing to grip the forearm for balance.

He blew across my opening and gave it another kiss. "You want to come, baby?"

"Please, Boss Man."

He kissed me again, this time, delicately. "I didn't hear you."

"Please," I said louder.

He circled my throbbing clit harder, applying the

perfect pressure to drive me into a powerful climax that made me nearly yank the sheets off the bed. My nails dug into his forearm, and I barely stopped my hips from bucking. "Boss Man..."

He sucked me harder, making the orgasm stretch as long as possible. He made love to me with his mouth, his sexy tongue doing wonderful things to me. He blew then sucked over and over.

I thrived in orgasmic bliss, my vision blurry and my spine tight. My cheek was against the bed, and my ass was still high in the air. All I could do was breathe, feel the tenderness as it slowly left my body.

Hunt rose to his feet, grabbed my hips, and flipped me over.

I rolled to my back and watched him move on top of me, his muscular physique covering mine. He folded my legs against my body and positioned our hips together, his torso stretching far above mine. He locked eyes with me as he slowly slid inside. "Amazing pussy..." He moved all the way inside until every inch of his length was fully sheathed. Then he moaned.

I moaned too. My hands started at his stomach and slowly moved up, feeling the intricate lines of his body as the muscles separated sections of his physique. He could easily be an underwear model if being a business tycoon didn't work out. His chest was my favorite part. It was smooth with sleek pads of muscle. I liked to drag my nails over it to feel the powerful strength underneath.

Instead of thrusting into me immediately, he moved his face to mine and kissed me.

Slowly.

Softly.

Gently.

Our mouths moved together in gentle embraces, our lips locking and then breaking apart. He gradually rocked into me, his thick length pushing in and pulling out. His rhythm wasn't interrupted by our kisses, which were soft but quickly escalating. He would kiss me, pull away slightly to look at me, giving me the hottest expression I'd ever seen, and then kiss me again.

My arms circled his neck, and I pulled him closer to me, my fingers caressing his hair. I needed more of him.

All of him.

My lips separated his, and I moved my tongue into his mouth, immediately feeling our breath mixing together. I ground against him, taking his cock a little faster. We came together, broke apart, and then came together even harder than we did last time.

Our bodies burned.

Our fingers ached.

I craved more. He took more.

"Hunt..." I spoke into his mouth as my lips trembled. My pussy was already tightening around him, another orgasm rushing through me as the tide returned. My kisses stopped completely because all I could do was moan into his mouth, to stifle my screams so I wouldn't shatter his eardrums. My hands gripped his shoulders, and my body shifted and writhed beneath him. "God..."

"Baby..." He deepened the angle and gave me more of his length, hitting me deep and hard. His tight ass clenched, and he buried himself far as he released with a quiet moan, pumping me with his come.

I loved feeling his come inside me. Made me feel like a woman, feeling a man's desire deep inside me. And not just any man—but Diesel Hunt. "Feels so good..."

"I've got plenty more."

MY MEN CARRIED MY SUITCASES ONTO THE PLANE, ALONG with the gown that needed to be handled perfectly so it wouldn't get wrinkled. I got out of the back seat once Thorn's BMW pulled onto the tarmac. He got out of the back seat, wearing slacks and a collared shirt along with dark sunglasses. "Beautiful day to fly."

"Yep."

His men carried his bags onto the plane as he

walked up to me. "Ready to get going?"

"I'm waiting for—"

A blacked-out Mercedes pulled up, and once the car was at a stop, Hunt stepped out. In black jeans and a black t-shirt, he looked suave and sexy with his aviator sunglasses he had on. He wore a dashing smile, probably pleased by the shocked expression on Thorn's face.

"I was about to tell you that Hunt was coming along." Little late now, but Thorn got the picture.

Thorn crossed his arms over his chest as he watched Hunt walk toward us. "Why?"

"He said he didn't want me to be gone all weekend. At first, he told me I had to stay. But I said I couldn't do that because I'd already committed to this before we were together, so he said he was coming along. Not much I could do about it."

Thorn's expression didn't change, but I knew he wasn't happy about this. "Is he staying at my parents' place too?"

"We're staying at a hotel."

"And what am I supposed to tell my mother?"

"Say I have meetings at the hotel. She'll believe that."

Thorn didn't argue, but his eyebrows were furrowing even more by the second.

Hunt reached us, his boyish smile on his lips. He

didn't greet me with a kiss because we were in public, but he didn't shy away from wrapping his arm around my waist and giving me an affectionate hug. His face turned into my neck, and he gave me a quick kiss just behind the ear, doing it discreetly so no one would notice.

I thought about last night, the way we moved together slowly until sometime in the morning. He pumped me full of his come and refused to let me shower so I'd have to sleep with it inside of me.

Pretty hot.

Hunt turned to Thorn and extended his hand. "Mr. Cutler."

Thorn looked like he might not shake his hand.

I shot him a glare, not sure what the problem was.

Thorn finally finished the gesture. "Didn't realize you were joining us."

"I didn't realize either until yesterday," Hunt said simply. "But where my woman goes, I go."

I wasn't his woman, but I didn't correct him in front of Thorn.

"Your woman?" Thorn couldn't sheathe his anger this time. He pivoted his body, naturally turning defensive, his shoulders appearing broader. The men were busy loading the plane and preparing for takeoff so they couldn't overhear this tense conversation.

"I'm the one sleeping with her, aren't I?" Hunt challenged.

Thorn stepped closer to him. "She's yours for the next five weeks. But she's mine for the rest of my life." Thorn was just inches from him, but luckily, he never raised his fist. He gave Hunt a ferocious glare before he walked to the stairs and boarded the plane.

Hunt didn't drop his smile, brushing off the feud like nothing happened at all. "Shall we?"

Hunt did nothing wrong to provoke Thorn, but I was disappointed they weren't getting along. Every time I talked to Thorn about it, he seemed to calm down. But when they were together again, tensions rose.

Hunt picked up on my disappointment. "If you think I'm gonna let someone talk to me like that, you wouldn't be fucking me."

No, I probably wouldn't.

"Let's get going."

WE CHECKED IN TO THE HOTEL. THORN ENDED UP STAYING at the same place because he couldn't stay with his parents while I stayed at the hotel alone. That wasn't believable, and it would probably make them think we were having problems.

We were both on the top floor, but at opposite ends of the hotel—on purpose.

I doubted Thorn wanted to hear us have sex all night.

"We're meeting my parents for dinner at six." Thorn spoke to me as we rode the elevator to the top floor. Hunt stood on the other side of me, being silent so we could have our conversation. "I'll pick you up at five thirty."

"Okay."

The doors opened, and all three of us stepped out.

Hunt grabbed my hand and pulled me in the other direction right away, taking me away from Thorn the second he got a chance.

Thorn let it go and headed the opposite way.

We were quiet in the hallway until we walked into the presidential suite. It was far too big for just two people, but both of us always needed to make a statement. Our luggage was already there, along with a chilled bottle of champagne and fresh flowers.

Hunt checked out the view of the Windy City before he pulled his shades off his face and set them on the table. "How long will you be gone tonight?"

"Not sure. His parents talk a lot."

I slipped off my heels and let my flat feet rest on the hardwood floor.

"Do you ever wonder if Thorn's feelings for you are more romantic than they seem?" Hunt slid his hands into his pockets as he looked out the window, his strong back opening wide into his broad shoulders.

"They aren't."

"And you're so certain of that?"

"Absolutely." I walked to the bar and made myself a drink. "He's possessive of me because I'm an asset to him. He sees me as his property even though we aren't married yet. There's nothing romantic about it."

"And you really believe that?"

"Completely."

Hunt turned around and stared at me. "Have you ever asked him?"

"I don't need to. If he felt that way, he would tell me."

"And what would you do if he did?"

I tossed the cherry and orange peel into the drink. "Nothing."

"Nothing?" he asked.

"His feelings wouldn't change anything."

"It would go against all the reasons why you're marrying him in the first place."

"Romantic love wouldn't change our friendship or loyalty."

"Would you return those feelings?" His eyes scrutinized every inch of my face.

"No. I don't see him that way. And this is a stupid conversation because he doesn't see me that way either. Thorn Cutler is not the kind of man who feels anything more than lust and power. He's very simple."

Hunt stared at me for several more heartbeats before he turned back to the window.

"This discussion is over. I have nothing more to say about it, and I'm not taking questions."

"This isn't a press conference," he said coldly. "And if it is, I'm running the show. I can ask whatever I damn well please."

I finished my drink then took a seat on the couch.

Hunt turned around and looked at me, his hand resting in his pockets.

I stared back, my gaze unflinching.

He pulled his hands out of his pockets and took the seat beside me on the couch. He took my glass out of my hand, took a long drink, and then returned it.

"Yes, help yourself…"

"I will." He rested his arm over the back of the couch.

"So, we have two hours before I need to start getting ready. What should we do?"

"I already know what I want to do." He turned his face toward mine, a devilish look in his eyes.

"And what's that?" I drank from my glass, letting the whiskey settle deep inside my stomach.

"Stuff you with come—in every single opening."

Hunt made good on his word.

He came in my mouth, my pussy, and my ass. When I tried to brush my teeth before dinner, he snatched the brush away and threw it on the counter.

Psychopath.

I got dressed, putting on a black cocktail dress with tie-dye shoes. There was a black lining along the edges, making them complement my dark dress. I pinned my hair to the side and pulled it over one shoulder, leaving it in loose curls but wearing it casually.

When I walked into the living room, Hunt was sitting at the table working on his laptop. His head was propped against his hand and he didn't move an inch when I entered, but his eyes shifted to me.

He checked me out—from head to toe.

"Like what you see, Boss Man?"

He gave a nod that was almost imperceptible.

I grabbed my clutch off the counter and tucked my phone inside. When I turned around, Hunt was already up and standing behind me. His hands moved to my hips, and he squeezed the fabric of my dress, making it rise up slightly. "Are you trying to torture me?"

"No. But if I am, I picked the right dress."

He released a quiet growl right against my ear. "You're lucky you're about to walk out the door."

"My boss doesn't care whether I am or not." I brushed him off by walking away, and right on cue, Thorn rang the doorbell.

Hunt growled again.

I opened the door to Thorn, who was dressed in black slacks and a gray collared shirt. Instead of looking at me first, he eyed Hunt over my shoulder, as if he wanted to know where he was the second the door was open. "I'm ready."

"Great." Thorn finally shifted his gaze back to me. His eyes didn't roam over my body appreciatively. He rarely looked at me that way, occasionally complimenting my appearance. But that scorching attraction Hunt always showed was nowhere to be seen.

Hunt was dead wrong about him.

Before I could step out, Hunt circled his arm around my waist. He turned me into his body and kissed me on the mouth, a little too hard for someone else to witness. His hand squeezed me, and he brushed his nose against mine. "I'll miss you." He kissed the corner of my mouth, and the gentle affection nearly took my breath away.

I didn't think twice before my reaction came out. "I'll miss you too."

A slight smile stretched his lips, making one corner rise in a cocky but sweet way. "I know, baby." He kissed my cheek before he finally let me go. "Take care of her." He turned his cold gaze back on Thorn. "I want her returned in the same condition."

Thorn looked like he wanted to stab Hunt in the eye with a butter knife.

Thorn and I walked off and headed to the lobby, where a driver was waiting for us. We got into the back seat of a black car, the divider up so we had our privacy. The driver knew the address, so he took us on our way.

I looked out the window, knowing a tense conversation with Thorn was on the horizon. He had a thing or two to say about Hunt. I could feel the words before they were even spoken out loud.

"You know all those concerns I expressed to you a while ago?"

I kept my eyes focused out the window. "Yes."

"Well, now I'm even more concerned." He turned his face toward me as his legs stretched out in front of him. "The guy came all the way to Chicago just to bed you? He couldn't wait two days? We have a problem, Titan."

"I admit he's possessive."

"Way too possessive for a fling. And you're going

along with it."

"He is in charge. You know the circumstances of the relationship."

"But you like it." He stared me down with his ice-blue eyes.

I slowly turned my head so I could meet his look head on.

"Titan, you have feelings for this guy. It's obvious."

I held his gaze and didn't look away.

"Tell me."

"Hunt and I talked about it a few days ago, our veiled meanings hidden in the shadows."

"What was said?"

"Nothing concrete. Just...what our relationship is. He said we're more than friends, more than lovers. We have a connection. I didn't agree with him, but I didn't deny it either. We moved into dangerous territory, talking about what kind of future we could possibly have. But I told him I wasn't interested in love, despite how much I like him, and my decision to marry you hadn't changed."

Thorn's angry look disintegrated, but he looked even more concerned than he did before. "You like him?"

"Of course."

"But you like him a lot?"

"I do... There's always been something there."

"Such as?"

"I don't know. I just feel differently with him from how I do with everyone else. And I know in my heart... when this ends...I'll be disappointed. I know it'll take me a few weeks to recover. It'll be hard to picture him with someone else. I'm jealous when I see him with other women. He's jealous when he sees me with other men. It's natural, and neither one of us can seem to stop it."

Thorn's eyes fell in disappointment. "You're in love with him?"

"No. I never said that."

"But are you?"

So far, I'd managed to keep a wall of ice around my heart. Hunt had melted some of it, made it thinner and weaker than it was before. But he hadn't managed to shatter it completely. He'd earned my trust and my friendship, which were already impressive accomplishments. But I managed to protect that last piece. "No. I haven't allowed myself to fall that far. I don't want to be in love with him. My desires haven't changed."

"Are you sure?"

"Yes, Thorn. I still want to marry you."

"Then maybe you should stop seeing him. If it's getting this hard...it might be smart to walk away."

That would be the smart move, to get out before I could get in too deep. But after he fulfilled his end of the deal, I couldn't renege on mine. "No. That wouldn't be fair to him. He earned me. I can't go back on my word."

Thorn turned his gaze out the window again. "Be careful, Titan. You're already in pretty deep."

"I know."

"And I told you he felt that way."

"He's never explicitly said it."

He shook his head. "He doesn't need to, Titan. It'd be redundant."

"You think so?"

"I'm telling you, once the final weeks are over, he's not going to let you go. He's going to ask for more. And I'm afraid you aren't going to be able to say no."

The fact that I hesitated right then and there was alarming to me. I knew what I wanted, but now these feelings were making me lose sight of that. I was confused, unsure. Thorn and I had already laid out our plans for the future, and I couldn't compromise what we already agreed to. Love was temporary. It lasted a few months, sometimes a few years. But it always died out, leaving far more heartbreak behind than it was worth. I had to remind myself why I'd decided to marry Thorn in the first place. It was the right decision—for me. "I will say no."

I STEPPED INSIDE THE SUITE AND FOUND HUNT SITTING ON the couch. His laptop and notes were still resting on the table, but he'd obviously abandoned them when he decided to enjoy a drink and the game. He was only in his sweatpants, which hung low on his hips and displayed the deep V from his hips to his stomach. His chiseled chest was outlined and hard, and his body was a map of endless muscles.

I set my clutch on the table and slipped off my heels. "How was your night?"

"Just booze and work." He held his glass over the back of the couch, an Old Fashioned. He'd probably been thinking of me the whole time I was gone.

"Sounds like fun." I walked to the back of the couch and took the glass from his hand. I took a drink, noting the way he used more whiskey in his drinks than I did. And he skipped the cherry.

"How was your night?"

"It was fun." Thorn's parents were the kind of people who didn't act their age. They had a zest for life, loved to travel, and never saw themselves as people in their sixties. To them, age was just a number. They lived life to the fullest, like it could end at any moment. Thorn was close with his parents, something I liked about him. I didn't have a family of my own, and it was nice to see someone cherish what they had. And one day, they would be my family too.

"What did Thorn say about me?" he asked bluntly.

At least the two men were honest about their feelings for one another. "The same things he's already said."

Hunt turned his face back to the TV but didn't really seem to be watching it. "Your party thing is tomorrow?"

"Yeah."

"Can I come along?"

"You know I'm going with Thorn." I returned the glass to his hand and made my own drink. I made an Old Fashioned, making sure there was a cherry in it. I moved into the living room and took the seat beside him.

"I can go alone. It's gonna be a big party, right?"

"But it's not like I can be with you."

"There's a bathroom, isn't there?" His eyes remained on the screen.

"I told you I was busy this weekend. If you're bored, you shouldn't have come." His arm moved around my shoulder, and he pulled me closer to him. "I'm definitely not bored." He grabbed both of my legs and pulled them over his lap, pivoting my body so I was looking more at him than the TV. He curled his arm around my neck so he could take a drink, never taking his eyes off me.

"You could get a lot of work done while I'm out."

"All I ever do is work. That's the nice thing about having you around—you're a distraction. You're the solution to my workaholism."

"Anyone's who's successful is a workaholic."

"Thorn isn't. He's been fed with a silver spoon."

I didn't mind when Hunt spoke his mind about Thorn, jealous of my relationship with him, but I wouldn't let him talk about something he didn't understand. "You don't know him, Hunt. You're in no position to talk about the things he has or hasn't had."

Instead of being pushed away by the cold comment, he smiled. "My mistake."

I drank from my glass, letting the whiskey wet my mouth.

"You're loyal."

"Only good people are."

"It makes me wonder what you say about me when someone insults me." He kept smiling. "I bet if anyone said the slightest mean thing about me, your eyes would burn black and your mouth wouldn't stop moving. You would tell them off with that cool Tatum Titan temper."

"What makes you think I'm so loyal to you?"

"Just a hunch," he whispered as he nuzzled his face into my hair.

We watched TV for the next hour, enjoying our

glasses of whiskey without saying more than a few words to each other. It was one of the quiet times when we did something else besides screw. Like a couple who'd been together for years, we enjoyed the silence our companionship brought.

Once it was past midnight, we turned off the TV and got into bed. Hunt removed his sweatpants and slid under the covers, sticking to his side of the invisible line. I took one of his cotton shirts out of his suitcase and pulled it over my body, letting it fall to the middle of my thighs.

"I brought that just for you."

"You did?" I pulled the sheets back and got comfortable.

"Yeah. It's my gym shirt."

I narrowed my eyes.

His smile told me he was joking. "It's soft and comfortable. I thought it was better than sleeping in my collared shirts."

"That was thoughtful."

"Not really. I just think you look sexy in my clothes."

"So this was entirely selfish?"

He grinned. "Yep. Completely."

I turned on my side and faced him, surprised there wasn't any movement toward sex. We'd fucked for hours before I had to start getting ready for dinner, and once in between, but that usually didn't tame his arousal. He was like a sex machine that could go on forever. "No action tonight?"

"I figured you were sore. I did fuck you in a million ways this afternoon."

"True." I was a little sore. He stretched out every hole in my body.

"I'm tired anyway...had too much to drink."

"You get drunk alone?"

"I just get drunk when I'm depressed."

I studied the side of his face when his words melted into me. "Why are you depressed?"

"You were out with Thorn...with his parents..."

"That really bothers you?" I whispered.

He shrugged it off and changed the subject. "How many partners have you had?"

I didn't answer. "That's a sexist question."

"I don't mean have many men you've slept with. How many arrangements have you had? I'm not asking out of jealousy or judgment. Why should I be jealous of men who have come and gone after me? When we're together, I know I'm the only man you think about."

And even when we aren't together. "Ten."

"Ten?" he asked. "I expected the number to be much higher than that."

"Finding the right partner takes some time."

"And how do you find them?"

"Thorn usually helps."

His right eyebrow arched in surprise. "Why him?"

"He knows people..."

"Does he do these arrangements too?"

Since it wasn't my place to share Thorn's personal life, I didn't answer. "I'm not at liberty to say."

"So that's a yes," he said quietly. "Makes sense now."

I didn't give him any kind of reaction. "How many women have you been with?"

He shrugged as he released a deep sigh. "Damn...I honestly don't know. I realize that's a terrible thing to say...but I really don't know."

"Not even an approximation?"

"You don't strike me as the kind of woman to be jealous of all the others before you."

"I'm not," I said simply. "Just curious."

"Over a hundred. Probably one-fifty."

I couldn't even wrap my brain around that. It didn't surprise me considering how experienced he was. He didn't just know where everything went...he knew how to make me see the moon and the stars. "You've never been in love?"

"No."

"Not even close?"

"Nope," he said. "I've never had a connection with

someone other than screwing. There's flirting and laughing...but nothing substantial. Women only want me for my money or my fame. That's it. No one has ever asked me what my favorite color is."

I smiled. "What's your favorite color, Hunt?"

He grinned as he stared up at the ceiling. "Blue. What's yours?"

"Pink."

He turned his head so he could look at me. "Really?"

"Yeah. So?"

"It's a girly color is all."

"Well, I am a girl..."

"No, you're a woman. I imagined your favorite color would be red...something bold and primal."

"I'm not a bull."

He chuckled. "You know what I mean."

"I like red...it's nice."

"Anyway," he said. "I've never been against relationships. I've just never found anyone real. People think I'm some playboy that fucks around because I have money and fame. But I only do that because that's how everyone treats me. They think that's all I'm interested in."

"Why don't you prove them wrong?"

"How?"

"Do charity work."

He laughed like I'd said something funny. "I've already founded three charity organizations, and I'm also involved with dozens of others. The media prints photos of me with a woman on each arm, but there's never been a single article about my charity work. Because people don't care. I'm much more interesting as an arrogant playboy. They feed on my feud with my father like it's a soap opera."

I never found out what happened after Hunt beat out his father for Megaland. "Did your father say anything about that deal?"

"No. But my brother called me about it."

"Brett?"

"No. Jax."

He told me they hadn't spoken in years. "Really? What did he say?"

"Said my father was really pissed, and his pride was destroyed. So he warned me and said a war was coming."

That was disgusting. "Your father really is an asshole. How can someone be that petty?"

He shook his head. "No idea."

"What kind of war is coming?"

"I don't know. But I don't really care. My dad can do his worst. I'm not scared of him."

When I looked at Hunt, I saw a hard-working,

driven, and selfless man. He was aggressive and authoritative, but he was also gentle, considerate, and understanding. If he were my son, I'd be unbelievably proud. How a man could jealous of his son's success baffled me. Every parent wanted their child to do better than them. At least, that's how it should be. "You're right. You have nothing to be scared of."

"Has your mother ever contacted you?"

The question caught me by surprise. We were just talking about family so it wasn't out of the blue, but his bluntness was still surprising. "Why?"

"Once she figured out how rich you were, I assumed she asked to reconnect with you."

No, that never happened. "No." There wasn't enough money in the world to make my mom want to get to know me, unfortunately.

"I'm surprised."

"I'm not. When she walked away, she wanted nothing to do with me. Doesn't make any sense for her to change her mind about that."

"I'm sure she regretted it. Not right away, but eventually."

"I doubt that. But I don't hate her for leaving."

"You don't?" he asked quietly.

"She left me in the care of my father, who was wonderful. She didn't leave me on the street. And when she realized being a mom wasn't for her, she did the right thing and left. If she didn't want to be there, it was better for her to be gone. She would have resented me and acted out toward me. I would have been stuck with a mom who wasn't affectionate or caring. Some people judge her for it, but in reality, she made the right decision for both of us."

Hunt stared at me in silence, his eyes not blinking.

"Same thing with adoption. When a mother gives up her baby, people judge her for it. But if she knows she can't give the child the life it deserves, then she's doing the responsible thing. She's giving her child a better life. That's what love is."

His expression didn't change. "You're a lot more understanding than most people would be."

"I had my dad. And he was just as good as two parents. We didn't have a lot of money and I didn't have a lot of toys, but that didn't matter. We had each other—we had love."

Hunt slowly smiled. "Very good point, Tatum."

He hardly ever called me by my first name. No one did.

"And what if she came to you now? Said she regretted what happened all those years ago?"

"I don't know..." I'd never given it much thought. I didn't hate her. I didn't love her. I was indifferent toward her. I didn't need a mother growing up, and I certainly didn't need a mother now that I was a thirty-year-old woman. "It'll probably never happen, so it's not worth talking about."

"I'm sorry if I made you uncomfortable."

"You didn't." I realized it was the most open we'd been with each other, talking just the way Thorn and I did. I talked about the mother who left me, and he explained that his father was still a heartless jackass. We didn't share any of the same experiences, but we had a lot in common—heartbreak.

"Do you have these arrangements because of what happened with that guy ten years ago?" He asked the question bluntly, probably taking advantage of the openness of our conversation. This was something he wanted to know about, had asked me about it before.

I considered telling him.

He watched me patiently, not asking another question until I finally gave an answer.

"Yes." He already suspected it, so I didn't see the harm in confirming it.

He turned his body on its side and looked at me, his eyes soft. "Did he hurt you?"

I held his gaze without blinking, considering what my answer would be. I trusted Hunt not to tell anybody. I'd already trusted him with so much. But my tongue didn't move, and the words didn't form in my mouth. A part of me was afraid of what he would think of me. It was a stupid thing to be concerned about, considering Hunt was such a great man. He was never judgmental about anything. He was understanding and exceptionally sweet.

I shouldn't hesitate.

But I still did.

Hunt broke the silence. "If you don't want to talk about it, I can wait. I'm a patient guy."

He let me off the hook. He recognized my unease, and instead of pushing me for answers, he just let it go. "Thanks... I guess I'm not ready."

"That's fine. I'm here when you change your mind."

WHEN I WOKE UP THE NEXT MORNING, I WAS ON TOP OF solid rock. Hunt's chest was underneath me, and it rose and fell with every breath he took. His smell enveloped me, swallowed me whole in a big warm cocoon.

My eyes opened, and I realized I'd crossed the line in the center of the bed.

And I was all over him.

He looked at me with a smile. "Morning."

I moved off his chest, aware of where I was and the

fact that I shouldn't be there. I pulled the hair out of my face and slowly retreated back to my side of the bed.

Hunt's smile disappeared as he watched me. "For the record, I woke up this morning like this—with you on top of me."

He could have dragged me across the bed when I was asleep, but any movement would have stirred me immediately. I knew the only reason why I was there was because I put myself there. "Sorry..." I moved back to my side, rustling the sheets as I slid away.

"No need to apologize." His strong arms let me go. "I liked it."

I returned to my pillow and pulled the sheets to my shoulder, cold on this side of the bed where there was no body heat. All the warmth and comfort were left on Hunt's side.

Hunt watched me with that handsome smile. "Now that you're awake, why don't you come back over here? You know you want to."

I did want to.

He patted the mattress beside him, his hard chest calling my name. "Come on, baby. Don't make me ask you again."

My mouth softened into a smile, and I slid back across the bed, back to the place I'd slipped away from. My body met his warm flesh, my hand went to his bare chest, and I rested my face in the crook of his arm. I hugged his waist and wrapped my leg in between his thighs.

It was much more comfortable over here anyway.

His lips brushed against my forehead, his kiss affectionate and soft. "I slept like a rock last night."

I didn't wake up once. "Me too."

"My shirt feels even nicer when I'm not wearing it." He smiled through his words.

"It is comfy." I hadn't slept with anyone for nearly a decade, and now I'd slept with Hunt every night for a week straight. Now I was used to his breathing, could tell the difference if he was asleep or awake. I was used to the sound of his alarm clock in the morning. I was used to those hot kisses on my neck.

And I was used to getting laid first thing in the morning.

That was a luxury I'd gone without.

"I have an idea," Hunt said. "How about we stay in this bed all day?"

"I'm gonna have to pee."

He chuckled. "Except for peeing."

"And I need to eat."

"Room service."

"We still need to answer the door, and I don't eat in bed."

"We'll make an exception today—and I'll answer the door."

"And what are we going to do in this big bed all day?" I asked.

"You're far too smart to play dumb, Tatum."

My hand moved up his chest, and I felt the hard muscles of his body. Nothing sexier than waking up to a man that felt like a brick wall. I wasn't a damsel who needed to be protected, but I didn't mind feeling protected by him.

"We're gonna fuck all day. And talk in between."

"What should we talk about?"

"Sex."

I laughed because I knew he was being serious.

"Stratosphere, cars, trips, your favorite things…"

"My favorite things?" I asked.

"Yeah. What's your favorite thing to eat?"

"Salmon and salad."

He rolled his eyes. "That's a terrible answer. What would you eat every day if you were allowed to?"

That wasn't hard to figure out. "Pizza. You?"

"Steak."

"You're a red meat kinda man?"

"I'm just a meat kinda man. What's your favorite country?"

"Hmm…France and Greece."

"Country is singular," he teased.

"Well, I can't choose. What about yours?"

"If you can't choose, then you don't have a favorite."

"Fine...Freece."

He looked down at me, his eyebrows furrowed in confusion while a smile stretched across his mouth. "What the hell is that?"

"Greece and France...get it?"

He laughed right into my ear, the masculine sound deep and earthy. "Clever."

"So there. I do have a favorite. What about you?"

"Hmm..." He shifted his jaw from side to side as he considered. "Russland."

"Russland?" I asked. It took me a few seconds to decipher. "Scotland and Russia?"

"Yep."

"Really?" I asked. "I've been to Russia a few times, but it's always snowing. Too cold."

"It snows here."

"But it's always snowing there," I countered.

"And it's a million degrees in Manhattan in the summer. I'll take snow over that any day."

"I like the heat."

"Then you obviously are never outside."

"Neither are you."

He narrowed his eyes in acknowledgment. "Touché."

"What's your favorite sport?"

"Football. You?"

"Basketball."

"Really?" he asked.

"Really what?"

"You follow sports?" he asked in surprise.

I tilted my head up to give him an angry look. "Why is that surprising? Because I'm a woman?"

"No. Because basketball sucks."

I smacked him in the chest playfully. "Does not."

"So does."

"Basketball is pure entertainment. It requires a lot of skill and quick reflexes."

"And football doesn't?" he teased. "You think crossing an entire football field with humungous men chasing you down is easy?"

"Never said it was easy. They always have to stop and reset...basketball is continuous."

"Because the court is tiny."

"Tiny?" I asked incredulously. "Basketball players run a lot more than football players."

He shook his head. "You're a smart woman who knows a lot more than I do, but this...you don't know shit." He smiled down at me, telling me he was teasing me and getting a lot of pleasure out of it.

I smacked him again. "You're the one who doesn't

know shit."

"Since I'm a gentleman, I'll just let you think whatever you want." He grabbed the room service menu and opened it so we both could look at it. "I'm hungry. I'm going to get some pecan pancakes and orange juice."

"I've never seen you eat anything like that in my life."

"We're on vacation. Live a little."

"In that case…" I browsed through the menu. "I'm getting the chocolate chip pancakes with bananas, a coffee, and eggs, bacon, and toast."

"Now we're talking." He grabbed the phone off the hook and placed the order. "You can just bring it into the other room and leave." He hung up then turned back to me. "Food is on the way. What should we do while we wait?" His gaze slowly intensified as he looked down at me.

I decided to tease him. "Discuss why football is stupid and basketball is awesome."

His hand moved to my hip, and he squeezed me in a threatening way. "You're playing with fire, baby."

"Maybe I like getting burned."

His eyes narrowed then he rolled on top of me. His heavy weight shifted the bed, and his muscular arms tightened as he held his massive form on top of me. His thighs separated mine, and his heavy dick lay against my belly as he adjusted himself into position. He tilted his hips, the head of his cock moving to my entrance. Then he bucked inside me, pushing through my tight opening and sheathing himself completely inside me.

"Oh..." I was never prepared for how good he would feel. His big cock was the perfect size to stretch me the way a woman should be stretched. If he were any bigger, then he wouldn't fit at all. He pressed his face closer to mine and looked me in the eye, watching my reaction as he dug deeper and harder. "Mmm..."

His back straightened, and his body tensed as he listened to me enjoy him. "Tatum..."

My hands glided up his arms, feeling the hills and mountains of his physique. My thighs separated farther, and I pulled my knees toward my sides, giving him more room to slide deep inside me. "Room service is gonna be here..."

"Then be quiet." He started to thrust inside me, moving both of us together as he slid in and out, taking his time as his large cock explored me from beginning to end. He scooted closer to me, his hips barely pulling his dick out of me at all. He wanted to feel so much of me the whole time.

My fingers found his hair, and I held on as I kissed him, feeling the arousal all over my body. My fingers tingled, my toes curled, my chest heaved...everything felt so good. I could already feel my entire body tighten as I prepared to be swept away.

"Not yet."

My lips hesitated against his as I whimpered. "Please..."

He moved into me deeper, burying his desire far between my legs. "No."

My nails dragged down his back, and I bit my bottom lip, doing the best I could to obey.

Minutes later, the doorbell rang, and the front door opened.

I stopped moving, but Hunt didn't. He kept grinding into me, his gaze never leaving my face.

God, I hoped they couldn't hear us.

Hunt deepened the angle, rubbing his pelvic bone against my clit. "Now you can come."

Jackass.

The room service person set up the table in the other room, dishes clanking together and the sound of the water glasses being filled. If we could hear him this easily, then I imagined he could hear us as well.

But I wanted to come.

Hunt plunged himself deeper inside me, his length coated in my cream.

I couldn't hold on any longer. I wanted to wait until the room service attendant was gone, but Hunt was making that impossible. He fucked me in the perfect position, burying himself at just the right angle to make my pussy betray me.

I came violently, my nails cutting into his back as I bit my bottom lip. I suppressed my voice and locked away my moans like they were hidden away inside a safe. My thighs squeezed around his waist, and I buried my face in his neck. "Fuck..."

He fucked me a little harder, a little deeper.

God, it felt so good.

When the heat was at its peak, I didn't care about the man in the other room. I just cared about how wonderful Hunt felt inside me, how his big dick was doing such incredible things to me, how this man pleased me in a way no other man had even come close to.

I contained myself the best I could until the passion abated. My nails loosened from his muscles, and I stopped squeezing his hips. The blurriness cleared from my vision, and I looked up into coffee-colored eyes.

The room service guy walked out, and the door shut behind him.

Hunt grinned, but his eyes retained the same fire.

"Asshole..."

"An asshole you love having between your legs."

There was no denying that. "Yeah..."

"Your tits look amazing today. Might come on them."

I continued to rock with him, feeling his cock thicken. "Better decide soon…"

He eyed my tits again before he looked me in the eye. "Press your tits together."

I cupped my tits with my palms, pressing them tightly together with a prominent cleavage line.

"But fuck, I love this pussy." He flexed his hips and fucked me harder, his fat dick pounding into me.

"She loves you."

He moaned at my words, and after a few more pumps, he pulled out and squirted on my tits. There were mounds of come, the hot and heavy stickiness coating me. It filled my cleavage, sprinkled my neck, and trailed down my tummy. It was a lot, so much that I wondered how it would have fit inside me if he hadn't decided to pull out.

He groaned in satisfaction until he was finished, his dick pleased with the results. He stared at his accomplishment, obviously proud of it. "Swallow it." His cock softened as it lay against my stomach.

I dragged my fingertips across my chest then dropped them into my mouth, sucking it up.

Hunt didn't blink. "All of it."

WE SAT TOGETHER AT THE BREAKFAST TABLE WITH OUR food laid out in front of us. I usually enjoyed my meals while I worked at the same time since I was a slow eater. I grabbed my laptop, but Hunt's voice interrupted me.

"No computer."

"I was just going to—"

"You're on my time now, Tatum." He stared at me with eyes made of coal. They were dark and dusty, just like his ruthless exterior.

I returned it to the bag and walked back to the table, in his t-shirt even though my skin was still a little sticky. I sat down and faced him, seeing him look back at me, shirtless, beautiful, and terrifying. "Yes, Boss Man."

He drank his coffee then picked up his silverware. "The only reason why we're eating in here is because it is easier." He cut into his food and took a bite of his pancakes. "Damn, I haven't had pancakes in years."

"Me neither." I sipped my orange juice before I took a bite.

We ate together in comfortable silence, Hunt looking just as sexy when he ate as when he did anything else.

My phone rang.

I stood up to grab it.

"No."

I halted at the table, surprised his control went

so far.

"Whatever it is, it can wait."

"It could be important."

"Not as important as servicing me." He nodded to the chair. "Take a seat."

I lowered myself again, battling the annoyance that rose up my throat. I didn't like being told what to do, especially when it involved my work. It was probably Thorn calling me on a Saturday morning to talk about our plans for tonight. But apparently, that wasn't important.

The hotel phone rang.

It was definitely Thorn.

Hunt threw his napkin down and answered it.

"So you can pick up the phone?" I asked like a smartass.

Hunt glared at me as he spoke into the handset. "This is Diesel Hunt."

It must have been Thorn on the other line because Hunt looked even more annoyed.

"She can't talk right now." He listened. "Why? Because I'm fucking her, Thorn. She'll call you back when I say she can." He hung up.

Damn.

He walked back to the table, but he didn't head to his seat. He came to mine instead.

"What?"

"Up."

"You just told me to—"

"Stand up."

I rose to my feet, unsure what he was going to do when he looked that angry.

"Bend over."

Was he going to make good on his word to Thorn and do what he said he was doing? I leaned over the table.

He smacked his large hand hard against my ass, spanking me with momentum.

I lurched forward, losing my breath because I hadn't been expecting the rough hit.

Hunt walked back to his side of the table like nothing happened. "Don't talk back to me again, Titan."

I rubbed my ass, knowing it was already red.

"You may sit now."

I lowered myself into my chair, in pain but also aroused. I hated the way he controlled me, but I admired him for it at the same time. He did it so effortlessly, so flawlessly. He took charge like a man who knew exactly what he was doing. He punished me for a crime that deserved to be punished.

I liked it.

And I hated it.

5

HUNT

We spent the afternoon in bed, exactly where I planned to spend my day with her. There was talking, sex, more talking, but mostly sex. Her ass cheek was still red from where I'd smacked it, and I liked to stare at it while I pounded into her from behind. I wanted her full of my come, my essence deep within her while she mingled with Chicago's finest.

When evening arrived, she left the bed, her hair a complete mess. "I need to start getting ready."

I sat up with my back against the headboard, my body tight from the intense exercise I'd had during the day. My ass was tense from pounding into her for hours. I made her come five times before I finally felt satisfied.

She continued to stare at me like she'd just asked me a question. She was looking for permission without actually asking for it.

"Then get ready."

She walked into the bathroom, her ass tight and her long legs perfectly sculpted. She had a thigh gap between her legs because even those muscles were tight. For a woman who didn't step inside a gym, she sure looked fit.

She shut the door and then the water turned on.

At that same moment, the doorbell rang. I didn't order room service, and I put the Do Not Disturb sign outside so no one would bother us.

So that meant only one person was at the door.

I pulled on my sweatpants but purposely left off my shirt. Tiny marks from Titan's nails were in my pectorals, and every lean and toned muscle made my physique undeniably perfect. I ran in the morning before work and lifted weights in the evening. Unlike Titan, I looked like this with a lot of effort.

And I wanted that jackass to know it.

I opened the door and came face-to-face with the blue-eyed man Titan had promised herself to. He was my height and of similar build. He was equally handsome but with different features. His jaw wasn't as hard as mine, and his light-colored eyes gave him a pretty-boy look. I was tall, dark, and terrifying. "Yes?"

Thorn didn't hide his disdain, his eyes narrowed in annoyance. "Where is she?"

"In the shower."

"I need to talk to her."

"Well, looks like you can wait."

Thorn took a step inside.

My hand went to the doorframe and kept him out. "You can wait in the hall."

Now Thorn looked like he wanted to punch me. "I'm not the kind of guy you want to fuck with, Hunt."

"What a coincidence. Neither am I."

His powerful arms hung by his sides, but they were about to launch at my face at any moment.

"I'll tell her to call you when she's out of the shower."

"Why don't I believe that?"

"Hunt." Titan's voice came into my ear. She emerged behind me, the authority in her voice returning to normal.

I sighed before I turned to her. "Yes, baby?" I slapped on a smile, pretending everything was just fine.

She pressed her lips together tightly and walked around me. "Please come in, Thorn."

"I'd be happy to." Thorn spoke with a clenched jaw as he shut the door harder than necessary. He gave me another fiery look. "Can we talk in private?"

I couldn't keep them apart forever. Titan had plans this evening, and I couldn't get in the way of that. She never canceled her engagements unless she absolutely had to. I didn't have any control over that.

"Give us a minute, Hunt." Titan gave me her executive look, telling me our arrangement no longer applied.

Just to be an ass, I positioned myself between her and Thorn and kissed her on the mouth. It was a sensual embrace, the kind of kiss we shouldn't have in front of other people. My arm circled her waist, and I squeezed the ass I'd spanked so hard. "Don't talk too long." I released her and walked into the bedroom. The suite had different rooms, so I took my laptop with me and sat at the table. I took care of some emails, checked on my stocks, assets, various companies, and checked in with some of my regional managers around the globe. Work never slept, and now that I was spending so much time with Titan, I had to make up for lost time.

Fifteen minutes later, she came back inside in the same robe she'd been wearing. It was midnight black and made of silk, showing off the nice curves of her body. Her hair was pulled into a messy bun, and she still didn't have her makeup on.

I looked up from my computer, meeting her gaze with my own.

She crossed her arms over her chest and stared down at me.

I didn't ask what Thorn wanted because it was none

of my business—as much as I wished it were. "Yes, baby?"

"Why do you call me that?"

"Baby?" I asked.

"Yeah."

I gave her a malicious grin. "Because I own you, Titan. I can call you whatever the hell I want."

She couldn't stop the irritated look from filling her face. She wore a mask for the world to see, constantly appearing pragmatic and indifferent, but now I knew every little expression she made because I'd seen them all. I knew what was really going on in that big brain of hers. "You're only making Thorn dislike you even more."

"Am I supposed to care?" I didn't give a shit what that asshole thought. He could hate me all he wanted, but it didn't change anything. I was fucking Titan good and hard all night because she was mine. He wasn't going to own her anytime soon.

"I guess not." She crossed her arms over her chest. "But he is my closest friend. I would hope you'd make an effort to get along with him."

"Why would I do that?"

"Because we're business partners, and once he's my husband, you'll be seeing a lot of him."

"I don't care if you're married. I do business with you —not him."

"Why do you hate him so much? He's smart, charming, and understanding. The only way someone could dislike Thorn is if they refused to let themselves like him."

"You're right. I refuse to let myself like him."

"You could at least respect him—for me."

"I don't owe him anything. And since I'm in charge, I don't owe you anything either. I wanted to tell my friends that I was seeing you, but you refused to let me share that information with anyone. So, no, don't expect me to bend over backward for the people you care about."

When she didn't say anything else, I knew I had her backed into a corner.

I turned back to my computer. "You should get ready. I'm gonna fuck your mouth before you leave."

She cocked an eyebrow.

"That way, if Thorn kisses you—he'll be kissing me."

SHE WALKED IN THE DOOR AFTER TWO A.M., STILL LOOKING gorgeous with the diamond earrings hanging from her lobes. Her eyelashes were thick and dark, highlighting the natural emerald color of her eyes. She wore more makeup than usual, but everything contoured her features even more, making the shape of her face more prominent along with the rest of her pretty attributes.

And her body...enough said.

That dress hugged her petite waistline perfectly, showing the womanly hips I liked to grab when she was bent over in front of me, the small of her back that was deeper than the bend of a boomerang. Her long legs were covered, but the hint of their shape was forever burned in my mind since I'd kissed them everywhere.

I watched her from the couch as she set her clutch on the entryway table and slipped off her heels.

My laptop was open on the coffee table, but I'd stopped working hours ago. Now I watched one of my evening talks shows, drinking more bourbon than I probably should have. Something about her being out with Thorn made me drink more than usual.

She set her designer shoes on the table with her clutch because they were too expensive to leave on the ground.

For a woman who wore heels anytime she was in public, she didn't seem to enjoy wearing them.

She walked to the back of the other couch, her hands resting on the back. "How was your night?"

"Good. Got a lot done." I was in just my boxers, preferring to wear nothing when a beautiful woman could walk in the door at any time.

She eyed me on the couch, her eyes heavy like she was ready to fall asleep. She glanced at the screen then turned back to me.

"How was yours?"

"Good. Spent time with other members of Thorn's family and a few other business acquaintances."

Sounded like a snoozefest to me. When she walked in the door, I'd intended to fuck her before bed, but noticing how tired she was made me second-guess it. Something about her being sleepy made her look vulnerable, and since I liked that look, I didn't want to chase it away. I liked Titan, the fierce woman who had a big brain and a smart mouth, but I liked Tatum more... because very few people knew her. She was quiet, contemplative, and open. She was sweet, affectionate, and so soft.

I turned off the TV and left my drink on the coffee table. I joined her on the other side of the couch and came up behind her, wrapping my arms around her waist and resting my face in her neck. I breathed in the smell of her perfume, the scent she sometimes wore to special functions. Normally, a light aroma of vanilla accompanied her skin from her body soap. It was subtle but fragrant.

I moved my hands up and down her arms, feeling the soft skin. My lips rested near her neck, and I listened to her breathe. It was impossible for me to be this close to her without wanting her. I could easily lift up her dress and grab her by the back and bend her over.

But I didn't.

I reached for the zipper at the back of her dress and pulled it to the top of her ass. The fabric slowly broke apart, falling over her shoulders and slipping down her body. Without my help, it fell to the floor, revealing her in just her black thong.

I could take a bite out of that ass.

Her breathing increased now that we were both in our underwear. She didn't turn around, waiting for my direction.

My arms scooped her up, bringing her to my body, and I carried her into the bedroom. Her arms circled my neck, and she let me carry her like a man carried his wife to bed. I set her on the bed before I got under the covers beside her. The lights were already off, so all I had to was get into bed.

I turned on my side and looked at her.

She was staring at me, her green eyes peeking behind her eyelashes. Her tits were covered by her arms, but the sexy line of her body disappeared under the sheet. She watched me like she expected something to happen.

My hand moved across the bed until I found hers. I intertwined our fingers without shifting my gaze.

Her thumb brushed over mine. "I thought about you a lot tonight."

"You did?"

"Yeah..."

I'd assumed I was the last thing on her mind after the day we had. She'd been my slave all afternoon as I fucked her how and when I wanted. Her lips were swollen because I'd kissed them so many times. She didn't get a chance to even open her computer because I commanded every single moment of her attention. "And what were you thinking about?"

"I missed you..." Her thumb stopped moving over mine, and she broke eye contact.

I didn't look away.

"I was with you all day, and you even pissed me off... but I still missed you. I wished it was your hand that was on the small of my back... I wished it was your hand in mine."

I wondered if she had too much to drink that night. She was drinking before she left, probably had a glass in her hand all night, and now she'd reached the glass ceiling of her tolerance. Instead of being aggressive or disoriented, she became transparent.

I needed to make her drink more often.

I leaned over the bed and kissed her hand, my eyes on her. "I missed you too, baby." I kissed each of her small knuckles before I returned to my side of the bed, keeping my distance so she could fall asleep in peace. "I always miss you."

"Do you?" she whispered.

"Yes."

She closed her eyes and loosened her grip. "Diesel..."

I loved hearing my name on her lips. Very few had the privilege of saying it. Jax said it to me on the phone the other day, but he was family. By birth, he was allowed to say it.

She didn't open her eyes again, but she tugged gently on my arm.

"You want me to cross the line?"

She nodded. "Yes."

I moved over the line and tangled our bodies together. I pulled her flush against my chest, hooked her leg around my waist, and rested my lips against her forehead. We were a web of limbs and torsos, our hearts beating together in the exact same rhythm. Our chests rose and fell together.

It was the most peaceful moment I'd ever known.

I didn't think about anything outside the two of us. I only thought of this woman, the one person in the world who knew me better than most. And I knew as many secrets about her. This had started off as pure lust, but now I couldn't deny how fond I'd grown of her. I cared about this woman, her happiness and her pain. I always had her back against the world—and her front.

I had all the money in the world. I had all the material possessions I could ever want. My life was simple. But it was also empty and boring. For the first time in my life, I felt excitement, a kind of high that hadn't faded away. I felt fulfilled, like there wasn't a single thing missing.

I felt complete.

WE PACKED OUR BAGS AND HEADED BACK TO NEW YORK.

When Thorn was with us, he was a barrier to our connection. I didn't feel as close to her, having to share her with this man she'd known longer. They were each other's confidant, able to say anything to each other. Titan and I already had that relationship, but in a preliminary stage. If we gave it enough time, I was convinced she would pour her heart out to me in a way she never could with him.

At least, that's what I hoped.

We returned to the city, and Thorn took his own vehicle back to his apartment.

I'd spent the last three days with Titan consistently, so I should head back to my place and prepare for the upcoming week. But the only place I wanted to be was with her.

The guys loaded our luggage into the cars, and we spoke to each other before leaving.

"Are you heading home?" she asked.

I searched her face, trying to figure out what she wanted. Did she want me to stay? Did she want me to leave? Did it really matter what she wanted when I was calling the shots? "I should probably head home and get some work done.

She nodded, but the disappointment filled her eyes.

"Unless you want me to stay."

She quickly hid her reaction like it had never happened in the first place. "No. I'll see you tomorrow, Hunt." She turned away to her car.

I grabbed her hand and pulled her back toward me, not caring if anyone saw us together. "I'll stop by in a few hours."

This time, she didn't hide her reaction. Instead, she smiled.

I walked inside Stratosphere and took the elevator to the top floor. Whenever I walked into work, I was usually devoid of emotion. I wasn't excited or disappointed by the prospect. It was just another day at the office, another day to make money and strengthen my reputation.

But whenever I walked into Stratosphere, I felt something different.

Knowing she would be there.

Tatum Titan, CEO of Stratosphere.

Co-CEO.

I felt the drumming of my heart, the flush of my skin, and the excitement in my pants. My eagerness didn't only stem from my attraction. She was my favorite person in the world—and I always looked forward to seeing her.

I saw her last night—but that didn't dampen my joy.

The elevator doors opened, and I walked onto the remodeled floor. We each had two assistants in the center of the room, each working at white desks that Titan had picked out. The office had a similar feel to the one she had in her own building, but she went out of her way to make it more masculine, knowing I owned half of this company. She did my office the same way, in the exact same tones as my penthouse.

I didn't go straight to her office. Instead, I walked

into mine and handled her emails and messages. I knew she was already there because her office door on the opposite side was wide open. For someone so fiercely private, she didn't like barriers between her and her working space.

I needed lots of privacy.

After an hour, I walked across the room, ignoring the looks all four assistants gave me, and stepped inside her office.

But I shut the door.

She looked up from her laptop, wearing a white blouse with a tight pencil skirt. Her hair was pulled back today, in a sleek updo that made her appear more professional but just as feminine. A vase of flowers sat on her desk, pink peonies. "Good afternoon, Mr. Hunt." She spoke to me like someone could be eavesdropping.

I didn't care if anyone was listening in. I wanted the world to know she was mine. If only she felt the same way. "I just went through everything you sent my way. I like the changes, but I think we should keep the presentation more traditional. It's not original, I admit, but if we don't compete with the sleekness of our retailers, then people won't take us seriously. Carol already did a shitty job running this place. Now we have to overcome that as well. Our rebranding should be as classy as possible." I lowered myself into the seat in front of her desk and rested my ankle on the opposite knee. I'd rather be kissing her as she straddled my hips, but we'd agreed to be professional when we were in the office.

Even though professionalism was overrated.

Titan stared at me as she considered what I said, her eyes glued to mine. She had a remarkable talent for sorting through complex ideas without ruining the intimacy between her and the person she was speaking with. She held dominion easily, pausing without losing confidence. "You're right. I agree."

"I'll get started on that."

"Okay." She turned back to her computer like our discussion was over. She was back to being Titan, the fierce and focused executive.

Tatum was nowhere in sight, not that I should expect her between the hours of eight and five.

I rose to my feet. "I'm heading back to my office. You know where to find me."

"Okay."

I didn't look back before I walked out, knowing she wasn't looking at me anyway.

I HAD A MEETING WITH MY OFFICIALS AND EXECUTIVES. My focus had always been on growing, making my businesses expand as much as possible. But lately, I'd been in a ruthless tycoon mood. I was buying small companies and flipping them, and I was growing Megaland at an insane rate.

I worked like there was no time to waste.

My goal was to be the richest man in the world, to pass the few men higher on the list—including Thorn Cutler.

I didn't want that man to have any leverage over me. He inherited a hundred-year-old company, not doing a damn thing to earn it. I, on the other hand, did everything from the ground up. I was a true entrepreneur, making my own wealth and growing it. I was a man who stood on my own two feet, not on the bones of my ancestors.

I was in my office when Brett texted me.

Let's get a beer tonight.

I kept in touch with my brother as often as my friends. He was the person I spent the holidays with, the one person in my life that was truly family. We were only half related, but I felt more related to him than I did Jax. In the back of my mind, I thought about Titan. I'd probably see her tonight, but I couldn't blow off my brother. *Sure. 6?*

Yeah. You know the place.

After I finished my workout at the gym, I showered

and changed before joining him at the sports bar. He was already there with a tall glass of beer in front of him. He'd already ordered me a scotch because it was sitting on my side of the table.

"Better not have put anything in my drink."

Brett rolled his eyes. "If I wanted to kill you, I'd use my bare hands."

"True." I took a long drink as I stared at him across the table. He was in a gray t-shirt and jeans, sporting a beard due to his laziness. "What's new with you?"

"Working on a new idea for a car."

"Already?"

"Yep. I was working on the idea for the Bullet years ago."

"You gonna give me one of those too?" I asked.

"Hell no, cheap ass. You're gonna have to buy one."

"Damn." I chuckled before I took a drink.

"So, how's it going with your lady?"

Of course that would come up. "Good." I didn't kiss and tell when it came to Titan. She valued her privacy like businessmen valued their bank accounts. I couldn't tell him the details like I could with other women. As a famous face, she had a sterling reputation to protect. It was stupid that it had to be that way, but I understood.

"Good?" he asked. "That's all you're going to give me?"

"You asked how it was going. I answered."

He rolled his eyes. "Are you still hooking up? Are you serious? Is this going somewhere? That's what I'm asking."

"I told you it was a fling."

"Flings last two weeks, tops," Brett said. "This is not a fling."

It started off as one, but it'd definitely taken on a new definition.

"You do business together...you're sleeping together...I know you like her...so what's the deal?"

"I already told you what it was, Brett."

His eyes narrowed. "And I think it's all a bunch of bullshit."

"When have I ever actually liked a woman?"

"Never," he snapped. "Which is why you never see the same one twice. But you've been seeing Titan for months. What does that tell you?"

I shrugged. "She's great in bed."

"No woman is that great. She's got a personality to boot, and you know it."

I hated it when my brother analyzed me. "Why do you care, Brett?"

"I care because I want my brother to be happy. And if Titan makes you happy, don't fuck around. Tell the woman how you feel, and be what she deserves."

Easier said than done. "She doesn't want to be anything more. That's the problem."

"She doesn't?" he asked in surprise.

"Yeah," I answered. "She still wants to marry Thorn."

"Even though she's been with you for months?"

I nodded. "She's not interested in love."

"Are you?"

I stared at him without blinking.

"Hunt?"

"What?" I answered.

"You want to be more than a fling, then?"

"Doesn't matter what I want."

"If you do, you should tell her. Come on, women like Tatum Titan don't grow on trees. They're once in a life-time. You want this woman, you fucking fight for her."

I could fight for her like a caveman, but that wouldn't change anything. If she didn't want to be fought for, then it was a moot point. Her arrangement with Thorn was ideal for someone like her. It protected her reputation, gave her a partner she could trust, and she would marry one of the wealthiest men in the world. It wasn't a bad setup. Arranged marriages were common for the rich and famous. "Brett, just let it go."

"I can't let it go if you're letting it go. I know you've been busting your ass with Megaland and buying all those other companies. You're growing your holdings by ten percent every single month. You've never been this ambitious before—and that's saying something."

"I like money. So what?"

"We both know this isn't about money."

It was about a lot more than that. "I feel like things have been different between us lately..."

Brett didn't say anything and finally just listened.

"It's not really about the sex anymore. We talk about things..."

"That's a good sign."

"But when I ask her about Thorn and the future... she still gives me the same answer. But every time, her hesitance grows."

Brett smiled. "I like where this is going."

"I think if I stay patient, things could change. But for now, I'm leaving it alone. It's not like she's marrying Thorn tomorrow. When our arrangement comes to an end in a few weeks, I'll say something."

"Your arrangement?"

I covered up my error. "Fling, whatever."

"Good. You shouldn't let a woman like that slip through your fingers."

"You're one to talk."

"How so?" he asked. "I've never met a woman like her. And if I did, you bet your ass she'd be mine."

"Like a woman like Tatum Titan would be interested in a man like you," I teased.

"We both know the women love me," he said with a smile. "And yes, that's plural." He drank his beer, a slight grin still on his face. "Like the threesome I had last night."

I rolled my eyes. "Thanks for sharing."

"I'll have to share for the both of us since you aren't sharing shit anymore."

I drank my scotch to cover up my silence.

"And that's how I know Titan is damn special to you."

"Why?"

"Because you actually respect her."

I WALKED THROUGH THE OPEN DOORS INTO HER penthouse, my bag over my shoulder. She was there to greet me, in just a t-shirt and her panties. Her hair was loose around her shoulders, and she wore light makeup, showing off her natural features. She smiled so big when she looked at me.

Fuck, my knees were weak.

She moved into my chest, wrapped her arms around my neck, and kissed me like she'd been missing me all day. Her look wasn't cold like it was in the office. She didn't wear that professional exterior she showed to everyone else. Her hardness faded, Titan disappearing and only Tatum remaining behind.

Tatum.

She moved her mouth with mine, her lips still stretched into a smile.

My hand moved into her hair, and I felt the warmth in my chest, my hands finally on the woman I'd been thinking about all day. My bag fell off my shoulder and hit the floor, but the sound didn't disturb either one of us. I smiled as I kissed her, unable to wipe the smirk off my lips. I'd never forget that moment, the way she looked at me when I walked through the door.

I wished she'd look at me like that every day.

She hiked her leg around my hip, and I grabbed the back of her thigh and held it there. My fingers dug into her toned flesh, gripping her tighter. My tongue entered her mouth, and I tugged on her hair gently.

She breathed into my mouth, her small teeth gently nibbling on my bottom lip.

I didn't interrupt our kiss as I picked her up and held her against my chest. One leg was already wrapped around me, so she hooked the other around my waist, her ankles locking together. I walked past the floor-to-ceiling window and headed to her bedroom.

We fell together on the bed, and I pulled her panties down. My jeans and shoes were kicked away, and she yanked my boxers off my muscular ass so I could get the rest away. She didn't bother with my shirt, and I didn't bother with hers either.

I slid inside her, and together, we took a deep breath.

Damn, it was heaven.

I held my weight on one arm so I could dig my hand into the back of her hair. I got a tight grip on the strands and rocked inside her, sliding my enormous dick into her ever-tight pussy. I'd been sleeping with her for months now, and that little channel never loosened.

I breathed against her mouth and enjoyed her touch. Her nails started at the nape of my neck and slowly dragged over my body until she reached the small of my back. She breathed harder and deeper, her petite body grinding against mine so she could get more of me. "Diesel..."

Somehow, I found that sexier than Boss Man. I didn't correct her because I didn't need to hear it. My spine tightened, and my dick hardened inside her. She called me by a name very few people had permission to use. But this woman had the privilege because she'd earned it. "Tatum."

Her hands moved to my ass, and she gripped the

muscle, pulling me deep inside her even though I could barely fit my length as it was. "Yes...I'm almost there."

I'd only started, and she was already shaking underneath me.

I ground against her harder, my pelvic bone rubbing against her clit.

"Oh..." Her hands lifted my shirt, and she gripped my muscular torso, her nails starting to dig.

I kissed her before she came, giving her my hot kisses and sensual touches. I danced my tongue with hers before I pulled her bottom lip into my mouth. "Come, baby."

She writhed underneath me, panting and screaming. Her nails made new scratches, and she squeezed my hips with her thighs and pulled me harder into her, needing all of my length as she constricted around me. "Diesel...yes."

I came inside her in the same moment, dropping all of my seed inside, filling her until there wasn't any space left. My favorite thing in the world was to fuck this woman, to give her all of my desire so it could sit inside her all night. I loved running my empire and reaping the rewards of the seeds I had sowed. But this was so much better.

She closed her eyes and rolled her head back, pulling me flush against her. "I love your come..."

"I love giving it to you." I tasted the sweat off her lips as I kissed her. My lips moved to her neck and her shoulders, kissing her harder than I had earlier. I sprinkled kisses along her collarbone, blanketing her in my worship.

Would she really want to walk away from this when our arrangement was over? Would she find anyone who could rock her world the way I could? Would she find this kind of passion, this kind of desire?

She opened her eyes and looked at me, her gaze heavy with satisfaction and exhaustion. Her hands migrated into my hair, and she felt the strands as she gently ground against me, feeling my cock soften inside her. "I want you again."

"Baby, you know I'm not done with you."

I STOOD BEHIND HER IN THE SHOWER AND RUBBED THE body wash into her back, touching her delicate shoulder blades, the long road of her back, and the deep curve in her spine. She was a petite woman, and I didn't realize it until I looked at her like this—completely naked.

In her dresses and heels, she seemed to be six feet tall. With her intimidating gaze, she felt bigger, stronger, more powerful. But in reality, this was all she was. Five feet something. I grabbed her arms and pressed a kiss to the back of her neck, tasting the remains of her shampoo.

She stilled at my touch, tilting her head forward so I could have more of her.

She invited me to kiss her, so I wrapped my arm around her chest and pulled her tighter into me. I kissed her shoulders, her collarbone, and her neck. My arms were twice as big as hers, my hands covering most of her body because they were so much larger than her petite frame. I wasn't hard because my body needed a break, but my mind was just as attracted to her as ever before.

And I just liked touching her.

She turned around and looked up at me, the playfulness in her eyes. "You're one hell of a kisser."

"Only when I kiss you."

We rinsed off then dried ourselves with towels. We didn't have dinner that night because neither one of us thought twice about it. We got into bed once we were done, Titan wearing the t-shirt I came over in. I put on my boxers then settled into her large bed, the large window showing the city outside.

The line drawn in the center of the bed was now nonexistent. She was either on my side, or I was on her side. I pulled her into me just the way I liked, with her leg wrapped around my waist. My face was pressed close to hers, close enough that I could feel her breath fall on my face when she breathed.

Now all of this was routine.

It was time for sleep. I had to wake up early in the morning and head to the gym before work. She was up at the same time as me, usually working on her computer while she had her morning coffee. Work was something we never needed to explain to each other. We were both passionate about everything we worked toward, and we both understood our businesses were our legacy.

I watched her heavy eyes fight the wave of sleep that took over. She was tired from her long day, tired from all the sex, and her body was betraying her. But somehow, she felt the urge and stayed awake.

A small smile formed on my lips while I watched her. "Can I ask you something, baby?"

"You always ask me things."

"Then can I ask another?"

"Sure," she whispered.

"Your publishing house...why won't you sell it?" Whatever her reason was, it wasn't a business one. It had some personal significance to her. It was a dying business, publishing going in such a different direction that no one had expected.

The sleepiness immediately left her eyes. "I hope you aren't still trying to buy it."

I chuckled. "No. I've learned it's not smart to do business against Tatum Titan, but rather, with her."

"Good answer," she said with a small smile.

I waited for the real answer.

"My father was a poet. He wrote short stories too. While he was putting food on the table, he tried to sell his work to publishers. He always dreamed he could make a living as a writer, so he could spend more time with me at home. That never happened for him...so I made sure his work got published."

I stared at her in disbelief, seeing the soft side of this endearing woman. She was emotional, affectionate, and deeply loyal. She never forgot those she loved, and she spent her life honoring them. The world had labeled her as a cold-hearted businesswoman, but she was so much more than that. She was compassionate, sweet, and painfully beautiful.

She turned over and opened her nightstand drawer. She pulled out a small book, no thicker than a hundred pages. She turned back to me and showed me the cover. It was a plain blue cover with ocean waves in the background. The name at the bottom read T. Titan.

"T. Titan?" I whispered. "Your father?"

"Tom Titan," she explained. "The first letter is an

initial because that's how he labeled all of his poems. I just assumed that's how he would have wanted it."

I took the book from her and flipped to a random page. Italicized words were printed, long poems about the pain of life as well as the beauty in it. I was dense when it came to poetry, but it wasn't hard to see the quality. In just a few pages, I felt like I knew the man who had made such an impression on the woman beside me, the woman who grew into the most powerful woman in the world. "He'd be so proud of you, Tatum..."

"I know," she whispered. "And I hope he's looking down right now...seeing all the people who bought his book."

"How does it sell?"

"Pretty well, actually. But then again...I publish very few other poetry collections. He doesn't have much competition on my shelves."

"Even if there were, these are the clear winners."

"Thanks. My dad was a great writer. Sometimes they were difficult to read...when he talked about the constant struggle for money, losing my mom, raising a little girl on his own...being diagnosed with cancer. His entire life is chronicled in this book. After he died, I got to know him a new way."

"Did you find this after he passed away?"

"No. I knew he was a writer when I was growing up. After I became a successful businesswoman, I decided to do something with it. No publishing house was interested in poetry, said it didn't make money. So I bought a publishing house and published it myself."

I admired her dedication. "You finished his life's work...but you're also his life's work."

"I wish he was still here. I miss him every day."

"I miss my mom too."

A thin film of moisture coated her eyes, but she blinked it away, making it disappear altogether. She grabbed the book and returned it to the nightstand. "It's nice that you understand...but I wish you didn't understand."

"I know."

She cuddled into me again, her arm resting around my waist.

"Thanks for telling me."

"Of course..."

My lips brushed against her forehead, and my fingers felt her soft hair. Her smell enveloped me, hugging me like a soft blanket. I was more used to her mattress than my own now. The rare times I slept alone were the nights I slept the worst. Now I was used to having her beside me every single day.

I didn't want to imagine my life when she was gone.

We had breakfast at the table together, sipping coffee and eating egg whites with greens. Most of the time, I didn't see her eat anything in the morning. She seemed to skip lunch too. And then she hardly touched her food at dinner.

I'd have to say something about it eventually.

She used her tablet at the table, already dressed and ready to walk into the office like a bombshell. She wore stilettos as tall as skyscrapers and a skirt so tight it lifted her perfect nectarine even further. She was a perfect ten wrapped up in executive clothing.

Instead of focusing on my emails, I kept looking at her.

She didn't look up from her tablet. "What?"

"I can look at all I want. That's what."

"But you must get tired of looking at this same face."

"Never."

She smiled before she set the device aside. She took one last drink of her coffee before she left the table and grabbed her purse. It was black and shiny, Connor Suede's logo discreetly printed on the side of the bag.

Piece of shit.

I picked up on her not so subtle hint and grabbed

my satchel from the door. I was dressed in my suit and tie, ready for another day at the office.

She walked to the elevator doors and hit the button. "I'll follow after you."

We didn't go down in the elevator at the same time anymore. Titan considered it to be too suspicious. "I'll see you later." My arm circled her waist, and I leaned in and gave her a kiss goodbye. It was short and right to the point, but it was still a nice way to start my day. I walked into the elevator and rode it to the bottom.

A few other people stepped out of the other elevators and exited through the lobby, all executives heading off to work. The doorman opened the door for me, and I stepped onto the sidewalk.

And spotted Bruce Carol getting into the back seat of a blacked-out car.

That was the second time I'd seen him near Titan's building.

Was that a coincidence? Or not a coincidence? Before I drew more attention to myself, I got into the back seat of my car, and my driver took off. I wasn't planning on mentioning the first time I saw Bruce to Titan, but now that I'd seen him a second time, I'd have to say something.

Hopefully, it was nothing but my paranoia.

My driver stopped at the stoplight, and the red light

seemed to drag on forever. I didn't have to worry about being late to the office because I was the one who made the rules, but I didn't like wasting time either.

I looked out the window and noticed a little bookstore on the corner.

"Circle the block and pick me up at this corner." I got out of the back seat, walked into the store, and browsed the poetry aisle until I found what I was looking for.

T. Titan.

I grabbed the hardback and opened the dustjacket. There was a small biography about T. Titan, and the picture was an image of him with a little girl in his lap. With dark hair in pigtails, she looked to be about five years old. He was smiling down at her, his glasses resting on the bridge of his nose. I could see some similarities between them, especially their eyes. They were identical.

I had my mom's eyes too.

I went to the register and bought it.

I was at work when Connor Suede gave me a call.

"Titan, how are you?" He spoke with a heavy, deep voice, his power radiating over the line. He wasn't only a fashion designer, but an astute businessman. He didn't just build a gorgeous line of clothes that men and women enjoyed. He also built an empire based entirely on his name.

"I'm well. How about you, Connor?"

"It's a beautiful day in New York City. And only beautiful things will happen on a day like this."

I was used to these strange philosophical lines he spat out. Sometimes they were extraordinary, and sometimes I wasn't sure what they meant at all. "I'm sure you're right."

"I was hoping we could do that shoot this afternoon —if you can make room in your schedule."

"I can make that happen. But should I do anything special with my hair? Get it cut?"

"Don't worry about that, Titan. My team will take care of it. Let's say we meet at three. We can get dinner afterward to discuss."

"Sounds good."

"My driver will pick you up. We're going to my warehouse in Brooklyn."

"Alright."

We hung up, and I went back to work. I'd only gotten through two phone calls with my regional managers in France when Hunt called me. He didn't call my work line anymore, going straight to my cell phone.

"Diesel." It felt strange calling him by Hunt anymore. When I thought of that last name, I thought of Vincent Hunt—capitalist douchebag. I thought of his estranged brother Jax, who hadn't been a brother to him at all. Hunt shared their last name, but he certainly gave it a new definition.

"Tatum." He didn't call me by my last name anymore either. Now it was always my first name when we were alone together. "You haven't come by Stratosphere today. Thought we could have lunch together in my office."

I knew exactly what lunch meant. "We need to remain professional at work."

"Unfortunately for you, I'm the one who gets to decide that."

That was true—but only for a few more weeks. "I have a lot to do here today. Could you handle the meeting this afternoon?"

"No problem."

"I'm leaving at three for my photo shoot with Connor."

Silence was impossible to hear, but Diesel's silence was loud. It was rough and thick, just like his voice. "I thought we talked about that."

"Yes, I remember." He made his feelings about Connor perfectly clear. He was jealous, and the last thing he wanted was for me to spend more time with him. "But this is a good move for my businesses—as well as yours."

"My businesses are doing just fine."

"But Stratosphere could use the push. That commercial with Brett was a success."

"But Brett isn't a douchebag."

"Connor isn't a douchebag either. I slept with him because he was handsome, charming, and respectful. I still think those things."

Diesel didn't like that answer. His silence made that clear.

"I'm not asking for permission. I'm just telling you what my schedule is for the day."

More silence.

"I don't understand why you're upset. Even if I weren't seeing you, I wouldn't sleep with him again."

"Why?"

"Because I don't want to. You're the only man I want to be with." I said that final sentence with more emotion than I meant to. It came tumbling out, like an avalanche down a cliff.

Now his silence was different. It was calm, and not a calm before a storm.

"After dinner, I'll be home."

"You're having dinner with him?"

"Yes."

He growled into the phone this time.

"Remember everything I just said."

"Baby, if I were having dinner with one of my super-model exes, you would be even worse."

"Would not."

He laughed into the phone like my statement was completely unbelievable. "Bullshit."

"I might be a little bothered by it, but not the way you are."

He laughed again. "Whatever you say."

"I'm not attracted to a man who's so insecure. You shouldn't be jealous of anyone."

"I'm not insecure. I just don't like my woman spending time with a man who clearly wants to fuck her —because he's already fucked her."

"I'm not your woman—"

"Yes, you are."

I got so angry that I didn't know what to do next. So my fingers made the decision for me, and I hung up on him.

Click.

I set the phone down and sighed through my teeth, frustrated by the conversation. Hunt was jealous of Thorn, and now he was jealous of Connor, two men I wasn't sleeping with. I admit I was a little jealous when I saw him with someone else, but not nearly in the same way. I went on about my day and tried to forget about the conversation altogether.

THE SHOOT WENT WELL. I WORE BEAUTIFUL CLOTHES THAT I would normally wear to the office, and I was photographed in poses that were rarely ever displayed. I took pictures in front of desks, in boardrooms, in front of expensive cars—

in every way that projected my success. I wasn't dressed in a short dress with my tits hanging out. Every outfit was classy, elegant. The images weren't about sex.

They were about power.

A few hours later, Connor and I went to an Italian restaurant in Brooklyn. He left his crew behind to develop the photographs and touch them up. Now it was just the two of us, talking about the clothes and the colors.

"I love that black pea coat. When I made it with my bare hands, I immediately thought of you."

"It was beautiful."

"And paired with that purple handkerchief...the perfect splash of color." He shook his head as his eyes took on a distant look. His thoughts seemed to rush by a million miles an hour. If I couldn't keep up with him, then I doubted most people could. He wasn't a photographer, but he controlled the shoot and set up most of the angles. "It's just..." He held up his hands then slowly lowered them again. "Absolutely perfect. Those photos will be so powerful. It'll change our perception of executive women, of fashion, of female power...that female strength is desirable...it is sexy."

"I hope the world views it in the same way."

"With photos as beautiful as these, they have to."

I suddenly thought of Hunt, wondering what he

would think of my photos. He would probably love them, even in spite of Connor's involvement. Hunt never called me back after I hung up on him. It was unrealistic to expect him to do anything after I'd pulled that stunt.

Connor went on and kept talking about it, immersed in the process even though we were already finished for the day. He never talked about us hooking up again or even gave the slightest impression he'd been thinking about it.

Hunt was jealous for no reason at all.

When we finished dinner, we said our goodbyes on the sidewalk with a handshake, and I got into the back seat of my car. My driver took me back to Manhattan and to my penthouse. On the drive, I scrolled through the business news and came across something that made my stomach turn.

Diesel Hunt spotted having dinner with ex, supermodel Paris Prescott. Are things heating up again? The couple had a short-lived romance three summers ago, and according to sources close to Hunt, he wasn't ready to commit. But perhaps things have changed. Below the caption was a picture of the two of them having a quiet dinner in a fancy restaurant. They were both drinking wine, and Hunt was dressed in my favorite gray collared shirt—the one I wore to sleep sometimes.

I felt something I didn't expect. Rage.

A lot of it.

Venom flooded my mouth.

I was so angry I didn't know what to do with it.

I knew this was a stunt to prove a point, but that just made me even angrier.

I rolled down the divider between my driver and me. "Change of plans."

THE ELEVATOR DOORS OPENED RIGHT INTO HIS LIVING room. "Diesel." I walked inside and threw my clutch on the couch. He might not be home, still out on the town with Paris, and if that were the case, then I'd wait for him to walk through the door.

So I could slap him in the face.

Instead, he walked down the hallway in just his sweatpants, his perfect physique on full display for me to see.

Paris better not have seen it.

He wore an arrogant smile, clearly enjoying how angry the whole charade made me. "You look upset." He walked around the couch and headed right toward me, his height towering above mine.

"I can't believe you pulled that stunt just to try to make me jealous. That's absolutely pathetic, Hunt."

"Try to make you jealous?" he asked with the same grin. "You *are* jealous."

"I'm not jealous—"

"Yes, you are. Your cheeks are redder than they are when you climax. Your eyes are like bullets, and I'm the target. You came all the way over here to give me a piece of your mind. Don't act like your heart didn't drop into your stomach the second you saw those pictures."

I crossed my arms over my chest, feeling my hands shake with anger. When I pictured him spending the entire evening with an ex-fling, it did make me sick. What else was there to talk about besides the sex they used to have? "I only spoke to Connor about business, not screwing on my yacht."

"I never screwed her on my yacht."

"Whatever. The place doesn't matter."

"Then why did you pick one?" he asked like a smartass.

I didn't want to look at him anymore. If I stayed, I would say something I regretted. "Good night, Hunt." I turned around and headed back to the elevators.

"Admit you're jealous."

"No." I hit the button and waited for the doors to open.

He came up behind me, his face close to the back of

my head. "Admit it, baby. I already know you are. I can't remember the last time I saw you so angry."

"No."

His hands went to my arms, and he gripped me gently. "I asked her to dinner because I decided to do a commercial with her for Megaland. Beautiful women who love tech gadgets will drive up sales."

"I didn't ask."

"And I've never slept with her."

My body stilled at that part.

"The media thinks we had a thing a few years ago, but we didn't. I was doing some private investing for her. I didn't want anyone to know I was in that sector because that's a conflict of interest. And since I don't fuck my clients, nothing ever happened."

The relief washed over me, and then a second later, the embarrassment.

He rested his forehead against the back of my head. "I don't need to look at your face to know how much better you feel."

I closed my eyes, finally feeling better for the first time since I'd looked at that picture of them together.

He kissed the back of my neck and wrapped his arms around my stomach. "You stormed into my apartment, expecting to see her here drinking wine on my couch while we swapped stories about our favorite sex positions...drove you crazy."

I felt stupid, but I also felt deceitful not being honest when the truth was right in front of me. "I was jealous..."

He kissed the back of my neck. "Insanely jealous."

"Don't gloat."

"No, I'm gonna." His smile was in his voice. "But I like seeing you jealous. I like seeing you go crazy when you picture me with someone else. Exactly how I feel about you..."

I slowly turned around and faced him, still keeping an angry face instead of showing my obvious relief. "But you have nothing to feel jealous about."

"You have even less to be jealous of. That didn't stop you." His large hands rubbed up and down my arms, his dark eyes sincere with emotions. "So let's stop pretending that we aren't fiercely possessive of each other."

"You only went out to dinner to piss me off. I didn't see Connor just to make you angry. That's the difference here."

"Alright, I'll admit it was completely intentional."

"Then, what was I supposed to do? Blow Connor off? He was doing me a huge favor."

Hunt stared at me, his hands gently moving up and down. His eyes remained on mine, dark and sexy.

"What was I supposed to do, Hunt?" I repeated.

His hands stopped at my elbows. "Bring me along."

"And what kind of explanation could I give for your presence?"

He moved farther into me, his forehead moving to mine. "The truth."

I stared at his lips as his hands gripped my elbows. The smell of his cologne was still on his skin, the scent he wore when he went to work and meetings. It usually wore off by the time he came home from work and rolled around in the bed with me. His sheets absorbed all of his natural smells, and that was the scent I liked. "You know I can't tell anyone the truth, Hunt. They'll think I'm two-timing, Thorn. No one will understand."

"Then break up with Thorn. Start seeing me instead."

"That doesn't make any sense either."

"It doesn't?" He pulled his face away and grabbed my chin. He lifted my face so I looked him right in the eye. "When this arrangement ends in a few weeks, you really think we're going to be able to walk away from each other? Fuck other people without thinking about one another? That we're gonna work together every day and not miss each other like crazy?" He looked at my lips again before he leaned in and kissed the corner of my mouth. It was a long kiss, a deep pause as our mouths came into contact with one another. I closed my eyes as the warmth spread through every inch of my body. "I'm not walking away. Neither are you."

HUNT OPENED HIS CLOSET AND PULLED OUT A WHITE ROPE, the surface smooth and sleek. I could see the light bounce off the material, giving it a slight sheen. He wrapped it around his arm then walked toward me on the bed, looking like a cowboy with a lasso in just his black boxers.

I sat there and stared, feeling my heart start to thump drastically in my chest. Ever since Hunt had been in charge, all of his tastes had been tame. He liked to control me, but he didn't enjoy hurting me.

I should have known that would change.

I reminded myself that this was different, that I trusted Hunt as someone very close to me. He cared about me, always put me before himself. He was compassionate, understanding, and the closest friend I had.

Once logic sank into my bones, I didn't feel scared anymore.

He stood in front of me, his ripped physique powerful and striking. He tested the rope in his hands, showing its obvious strength. "On your stomach."

I stared at the rope in his hands, drawing a blank. All I could do was sit and stare, thinking about that threaded rope tight around my wrists. I would be completely at his mercy, without any control whatsoever.

He looped the rope then tugged on both ends, making it snap loudly. "Now."

I finally cooperated, turning over to lie on my stomach.

"You're forgetting something."

I knew exactly what. "Yes, Boss Man."

He grabbed my ankles and straightened my legs until they dangled over the bed. He secured the rope around my ankles, tying them tightly together so I couldn't move unless I bent my knees. He took the rest of the rope and climbed on top of me. "Wrists."

I hesitated before I placed them at the small of my back.

He secured them together, positioning me tightly enough that I couldn't even move my elbows. I lay there with my cheek resting against the bed, waiting for whatever fun he wanted to have with me.

Hunt pulled off his boxers and kicked them onto the

floor. Then he held himself on top of me, pushing his fat cock between my ass cheeks. He ground against me slowly, moving through the soft flesh. He gathered the lubrication from my pussy and smeared it between my crack.

I didn't know what he was going to do, fuck my ass or my pussy.

Knowing him, it was probably both.

He hooked his arm underneath my chest and forced me up, arching my back and turning my face toward him. He kissed my jawline and made his way to my mouth. He kissed me softly, a direct contradiction to how roughly he gripped me now. "Tell me what you were thinking when you saw me with Paris."

My chest rose and fell against his arm. I felt his thick cock rest between my ass cheeks, twitching and throbbing as he yearned to fuck me good and hard. My bound wrists rested at the top of my ass, the rope rubbing against the small of my back.

"Tell me."

"You were wearing my favorite shirt...that gray one I like to sleep in. I hated picturing her wearing it."

"What else?"

"I wondered if she wanted to make a move...and if she would."

"And?"

"I felt sick to my stomach... I felt so angry...so hurt."

He kissed my jawline again. "But I'm all yours, baby. The only woman I want is underneath me." He nibbled on my earlobe before he let a hot breath escape into my canal. "Paris Prescott has nothing on you."

"You think so?"

He kissed the shell of my ear. "I know so. But now I have to punish you for going to dinner with that asshole. The only man you eat with is me." He released my chest and held his body on both arms.

My chest lay against the bed, my cheek returning to the mattress.

"Up." His deep voice sounded in my ear.

I raised myself up again, the small muscles in my back working to keep me upright.

He kissed the back of my neck and dragged kisses down my spine. His beard brushed against my sensitive skin, scratching me in the sexiest way. His mouth moved to my shoulder, and he gently sank his teeth into me, giving me a playful bite.

I closed my eyes and moaned.

He pointed his cock at my entrance then slid inside, moving through my slick pussy until every inch was sheathed in my lubrication. "You're always wet for me, baby." He breathed right into my ear as he started thrusting, his hips bucking against my ass. Every time he moved, he slapped my ass with his body, making a loud clap. My hands instinctively pulled on the rope binding my wrists together, but they couldn't shift even an inch.

Hunt groaned in my ear as he fucked me, sliding in and out of my cunt. "So fucking good." Every time he was inside me, he shoved himself as deep and hard as he could go, leaving his balls against my ass.

I pulled on the rope because I wanted to grip his muscular thigh. I wanted to feel that powerful body on top of mine with my own hands. But the grip was too tight, and every time I moved, the rope dug deeper into me.

He suddenly spanked my ass without warning, his large palm hitting with me surprising force.

I lurched forward and released a small yelp of surprise.

He rubbed my ass in apology afterward, massaging the tingling skin. "Your skin reddens so easily..." He thrust inside me again, his mouth moving to my neck. He kissed the skin hard and sucked it, becoming more aggressive with me. Then he spanked my ass again, his palm twitching in the movement.

I let out a moan.

He switched hands and slapped my other cheek, hitting it just as ruthlessly as the other.

I breathed through the pain, feeling the burn of both of my cheeks.

Hunt fucked me harder now, grunting in my ear as he rocked the headboard into the wall. He slapped me again and again, spanking me for the crime I committed. The hits were always unexpected, and he stuck me hard and fast, not giving me gentle taps.

My eyes started to tear up, the burning pain of my skin triggering my tear ducts.

Hunt looked into my face, watching the tears roll. "Just ask me to stop, and I will."

"Never."

He pressed his weight further on top of me and fucked me hard and deep. He shifted his weight back and forth, making my clit rub against the sheets underneath me. He stopped spanking me, giving me a break long enough to come.

And to come hard.

I tried to suppress my scream, but it was no use. It came out loud and sharp, echoing in his large bedroom.

Hunt's husky voice came into my ear. "Say my name."

"Diesel."

He thrust into me harder.

"Say it again."

"Diesel."

"Now say I'm your man." He thrust into me harder, making the orgasm stretch on for a long time.

I didn't hesitate because I was high from the climax, enjoying all the sensations he gave me. "You're my man..."

He groaned into my ear as he came, filling my pussy with all of his come. He pumped into me like a hose putting out a fire. He gave me so much that it seeped out of my entrance immediately. "And you're my woman."

HE CAME OUT OF THE BATHROOM WITH A JAR OF ointment. "Turn over."

I was on my back in bed, my ass still bright red from his smacking me so many times. "I don't need—"

"Now."

I had to be constantly reminded that we were playing by his rules now. If he wanted me to turn over, I had to cooperate. I pulled the sheets back and moved to my stomach. My wrists had light scratch marks from the ropes, but if I wore a long-sleeved blouse for the next few days, no one would notice the abrasions.

He grabbed my hips and adjusted my body until I was exactly where he wanted me. Then he squirted the ointment over my both of my cheeks and rubbed the gel into my irritated skin.

The abused skin immediately cooled off, a flood of relief sweeping over me.

"How's that feel, baby?"

"Pretty good..."

His large fingers rubbed the skin until the ointment was entirely dissolved, leaving a slight amount of oily residue on the surface. Then he pressed his face between my legs and kissed me, his large tongue gently caressing my clit.

I closed my eyes as my breathing deepened, feeling his tongue do incredible things to me. He'd just fucked me so roughly, and now he was caressing me like the wind against a rose petal.

Oh god.

His large hands gripped my cheeks, and he massaged them as he kissed me, giving me relief in two very different ways. His large cock had fucked me hard, making me so sore because he hit me so deeply every time. Now he was making up for it with his gentle touches. "You like that, baby?"

"Yes..."

He did that to me for fifteen minutes, making me feel good with light strokes of his tongue. He didn't push me into an orgasm, wanting to make me relaxed and feel good instead. When he was ready to push me over the edge, his mouth took me more aggressively. He sucked my skin and fucked my clit with his tongue.

I felt my body tighten in response, prepared for the oncoming rush of pleasure. He'd just made me come thirty minutes ago with his thick cock, and now he was doing the same with his lips. My mouth moved to the sheets, and I screamed into the covers, my moans only slightly muffled by the bedding. Now that my hands were free, I gripped the sheets around me and thrust my hips into the mattress, my body reacting in its own way. "Diesel..."

Hunt kept kissing me until I was completely finished, his tongue savoring my swollen parts as he tasted me. He pulled his mouth away then crawled on top of me, looking at me passed out on the comforter. He pressed his lips to my cheek and smiled. "Seemed like you enjoyed that."

"What gave me away?"

He kissed my cheek then the corner of my mouth before he got off me. "You hungry? Want something to eat?"

I'd been too busy climaxing to care about food. "Sure."

"I'm whip something up." He opened his hamper

and pulled out the gray collared shirt he wore to dinner. "You can wear this."

I eyed it before I pulled it toward me.

"And you can keep it too."

"Your shirt?" I whispered.

"Yeah. It looks better on you anyway."

I LAY ON MY SIDE IN BED BECAUSE MY ASS WAS TOO SORE. Hopefully, it'd feel better by morning so I could sit at my desk without placing a pillow under my ass. People would know I'd either been spanked or fucked hard in the ass.

Hunt lay beside me in bed, confirming his alarm on his phone and checking any extra emails that came through. The light projected from the phone lit up his face, highlighting the dark color of his eyes and his thick beard. He hadn't shaved today or yesterday, and now the hair was coming in heavy. I liked him either way, but when his jaw was clean, his eyes looked more formidable. I guess I preferred that hostile look.

He set his phone on the nightstand then looked at me. "Hmm?"

"What?"

"You're staring."

"I thought I could stare all I wanted."

"No," he said. "I said I could stare all I wanted. I own you."

"You'd rather I look at something else, then?" I teased. "Someone else?"

His eyes narrowed in a false sense of anger. "Better not. You know what you'll get."

"My ass is a little too sore for that right now."

"You want another rub?" He smiled, clearly proud of everything he'd done to me that afternoon.

"All I need is time now."

He turned off his bedside lamp then scooted closer to me on the bed. His arms enveloped me, acting as bars of a cage. He enclosed me in his warmth and smell, putting me in a safe place where no one could ever touch me. "Gonna take the day off work tomorrow?"

"I never take the day off."

"Not even when you're sick?"

"I don't get sick."

"When you take a vacation?"

"I don't take vacations."

He grinned as he looked at me. "That sounds boring."

"You don't strike me as someone who takes vacations either."

"I hop on a plane now and then. More often than you."

"Well, I like working."

"So do I," he said. "Maybe we should take a vacation together. Go to some remote island in the middle of nowhere and soak up the sun."

"That doesn't sound so bad."

"Just you and me and paradise—and sex."

"I figured."

He rested his lips against my forehead as he got into position. That was how we always seemed to sleep together, facing each other with his jaw against my forehead. Now I was used to having him beside me, was used to the way he breathed while he was asleep. I thought it would terrify me, elicit horrible memories that I wanted to forget, but it was only peaceful. "Good night, baby."

I softened against him, growing fond of that nickname. "Good night, Diesel."

———

THORN TEXTED ME WHILE I SAT AT MY DESK. MY ASS didn't hurt as much as it had yesterday, but it was still a little sore. I shifted my body a few times, relieving the stress on my cheeks when I could. *Hey, I've got this charity gala thing tonight. Need you on my arm.*

I was just on your arm last weekend. I didn't want to be out in public, talking about things I didn't really care about when I could be home with Hunt, one of the few people who knew who I truly was. Our conversations were natural and real, and even when we weren't talking, it was nice.

So? You're gonna be on my arm for the rest of our lives. I say you get used to it.

I never questioned Thorn when he asked me to go somewhere with him. I didn't mind going out and spending time with him. He was my favorite person in the world. But now, I didn't have as much interest. *I've been working so much. I just want to have a quiet night in tonight.*

Oh, come on. Don't leave me hanging like that, Tay.

Well, you invited me at the last minute.

I was invited to this thing like four months ago, but I totally forgot. I'm gonna hit up a few business tycoons while I'm there. It'll be a perfect networking opportunity.

I wasn't a fan of networking. It was difficult for people to take me seriously, despite my overwhelming success. To most men, I would always be just a woman and a dangerous partnership.

Come on. I'm sure you've got a beautiful dress in that big closet of yours that needs to be worn.

I smiled because Thorn knew how to get to me. *Not the point.*

And beautiful shoes to boot. I'll pick you up at seven.

I knew this was happening because I felt guilty for blowing him off. We were partners, and we intended to conquer the world together. So that meant we would have to attend stuffy dinner parties and collect tabs on all the people we wanted to overthrow. *Fine.*

That's my girl.

I got back to work then got a text message from Connor Suede. *I've got the photos. I'm going to swing by and give you a peek.*

That sounds great.

See you in about thirty minutes.

Having Connor stop by immediately made me think of Hunt and how he would feel about that. Having that man alone with me in my office would drive him crazy. He was jealous and possessive, but I quickly realized I was the exact same way.

Jessica's voice came through the intercom minutes later. "Titan, Mr. Hunt is here to see you."

Uh, why? If he needed something, he would just call. He wasn't stopping by for a quickie since my doors were made of glass. I didn't know what he wanted, but it better be important. "Send him in."

Hunt walked in the door a moment later, looking outstanding in his gray suit. The dark color of his hair and eyes contrasted against the fair material. His tanned skin peeked out from underneath his collared shirt at his neck. He made any color look great, but gray was particularly beautiful on him.

He helped himself to a seat and crossed his legs. No verbal greeting was issued.

I stared at him, keeping my legs crossed and my face emotionless. It used to be easy for me to be indifferent to him in public, but now it was a struggle. My first impulse was to rise to my feet and kiss him right on the mouth. My hand even twitched when he walked in the door, imagining my fingers stroking along his jawline. He shaved that morning, so I wanted to feel the smooth skin with my fingertips.

But I stayed in my seat.

He stared at me like I was the one who'd interrupted his day, not the other way around.

When it was clear he wasn't going to say anything, I spoke. "How can I help you, Diesel?"

A slight smile formed on his mouth when I used his first name. "I stopped by because I had some issues at Stratosphere. The patent that was applied for is still pending. Apparently, one of the lead engineers is having a copyright infringement issue."

"Idiot."

"I think it'll get cleared up. In the meantime, I met with our overseas shipment company. They're having a shortage of the material too, so costs are going to rise. I think we should rebrand ourselves to be more high-end. Right now, we live in a world of dollar stores and cheaper retailers. Everything is becoming flimsy and cheap. People want quality products, even if they have to pay a little more. I think that's the direction we should take. With your reputation as well as mine, people will go for it."

"You think?"

"Especially after your shoot with Connor."

Just then, Jessica spoke through the intercom. "Connor Suede is here to see you, Titan."

Did I have the worst luck in the world?

Hunt's eyes narrowed as he looked at the intercom. His expression turned even harsher when he looked at me.

Now I wasn't sure what to do. I didn't want to keep Connor waiting, but I didn't want to kick out Hunt either.

Jessica spoke again. "Titan?"

I looked at Hunt, keeping a professional demeanor.

"Can we continue this conversation later? I can swing by Stratosphere—"

"I'll wait." His hands came together in his lap, and his legs remained crossed. He didn't look as furious as I'd seen him, but the threat was still in his gaze. He was exerting his ironclad control to remain stoic, and it was working—for the most part.

"Outside?" I asked.

"No." He patted his armrest. "I'll wait right here."

Even if I asked him to leave, he wouldn't budge. I hit the button on the intercom. "Send him in, Jessica."

"Will do."

Connor Suede stepped in a moment later, a portfolio under his arm. His eyes were on me, ignoring Hunt as if he didn't see him. "Titan." He extended his hand across the desk.

I shook it. "Thanks for dropping by. I've been thinking about these photos for a while."

"Then you're going to be very happy when you see them." He was in a black blazer with a white V-neck underneath. The muscles of his chest popped out under the shirt, his tanned skin just as noticeable.

"Connor, you know my business partner, Diesel Hunt."

Connor turned to him, noticing him for the first time. "Of course. You wore one of my jackets to the

Naples fashion show in Milan. Beautiful piece of clothing."

Connor Suede paid great attention to detail. He knew if I was wearing his clothes just by looking at me. As the head designer, he was the one who meticulously combined all colors, makes, and patterns. His line of clothing wasn't extensive, but that was because he put considerable thought into each piece.

Connor extended his hand to shake Hunt's.

He'd better take it.

Hunt stared at it like he might not.

Even though Hunt wasn't looking at me, I glared at him furiously.

Hunt finally shook his hand. "I got a lot of compliments on it that night."

"I bet." Connor took a seat and opened the folder. "Check out these beauties." He set the first batch of photos on the desk.

I looked at each one, loving the pictures and the way I looked. They were all candid, but they seemed to come out the best. I'd enjoyed the way the clothes felt on my body, the way they hugged my skin. "They're lovely, Connor."

"That scarf was the perfect splash of color."

Hunt rose from his seat and came around the desk, looking at the pictures over my shoulder. "This one is my favorite." He pointed to me standing in front of a window in the office, a desk holding a laptop and coffee mug. I was wearing a simple black dress with my hair pulled over one shoulder. My face was angled, so only my profile was visible.

"You photograph well," Connor said. "If you lose everything tomorrow, there's always space on my runway."

Hunt's head lifted up, his eyebrows rising.

I collected the photos and returned them. "When will the commercial hit the air?"

"Next week. The advertisements will be in the next issue of major magazines. But you'll see a few on the billboards. People are going to go crazy for my fall line." He returned the photos to the folder then tucked it under his arm. "Thanks so much for giving this to me, Titan."

"I should be thanking you, Connor."

He smiled then extended his hand. "I'll be in touch."

I shook his hand. "Alright."

Connor shook Hunt's hand again before he walked out.

Hunt stood by the window, watching him leave until he was officially gone. Then he turned back to the view of the city, his hands resting in his pockets.

He was undoubtedly mad. I was spending more time

with Connor than he cared for. I didn't hug the man, but even a handshake was too much.

I took a seat at my desk and tried to brush off the hostility.

When he spoke, his voice didn't possess the rage I expected to hear. "Those photos really are beautiful."

I didn't turn around to look at him. "You think so?"

"Yeah. But I'm biased. I only love them because you're in them." He turned back to the desk and walked around my office like it belonged to him instead of me. "He leave you any copies?"

"Yeah. Right here." I grabbed the folder sitting at the edge of my desk.

He flipped through them until he found the one he wanted. "This one is mine now."

"And what are you going to do with it?"

He dropped the photo into the inside pocket of his suit. "None of your concern." He walked past my desk and headed to the door. "I'll see you tonight, Tatum."

I suddenly remembered the plans I'd made with Thorn. "It'll have to be late. Probably around ten."

He turned around, a look of pure displeasure on his face. "Why is that?"

"I have plans." I wasn't going to say what they were unless I had to.

"Better not be with him." By him, it was obvious he was referring to Connor.

"It's not."

"Then who?"

I didn't like answering to anyone. I prided myself on living a life where I was the boss of everything—including myself. But I signed my soul over to the devil, and now the devil himself was there making demands. "Thorn and I are going to a charity event tonight."

"The Manhattan Met Gala?"

"Yeah."

He came back to my desk, his hands in his pockets.

"I'll come by when we're finished."

"I was invited to that as well. But I wasn't planning on attending."

"Why?"

"Because I planned on spending the evening with you."

He made me feel guilty without even raising his voice. "I'm sorry, Diesel. I would blow it off, but it's important to Thorn that I go."

"I have the power to change your plans for the evening."

He did. All he'd have to do was issue the order, and I'd have to lie to Thorn and bail.

"But I won't. Just expect to pay the price when you get back."

———

THORN PICKED ME UP AT MY PENTHOUSE. THE ELEVATOR doors opened, and he stepped inside in a deep navy suit. "Yo, it's me."

I grabbed my clutch off the counter and snapped on my bracelet. "Hey." I wore a short cocktail dress, black with a hint of lace.

"Ready to raise money for the homeless...or some disease? I honestly have no idea."

Of course he didn't. "It's to raise money for the new community center."

"Oh...I think I remember that now." He adjusted his silver watch on his wrist and checked the time. "We should get going." He gave me two thumbs up. "You look damn fine, by the way."

"Thanks," I said with a smile.

"Your bulldog isn't here."

"No. If he were, you would already know by now."

We took the elevators down to the lobby then got into the back seat of the black Mercedes. The driver drove us back across town to where the gala was being held at a historic building with a great view of the park.

Thorn placed his hand on my wrist as he sat directly beside me. "I've been doing something thinking."

"That's never good," I teased.

He flashed his handsome smile, brushing off my joke like all the others. "My mom has been pestering me...and things have been moving forward so quickly. You acquired Stratosphere, and I've been working with that new lentil company."

I didn't know what point he was trying to make. I was aware of all his endeavors, as he was aware of all of mine.

"We've been talking about getting married for years now. I think we should just do it."

What?

"So, a month from tonight, I'm planning to take you to the fanciest restaurant in Manhattan. I'll make sure all the media is there. I'll get down on one knee and pop the question. I was thinking we'd have a summer wedding."

I kept staring at him, seeing his eyes light up in their usual way when he was excited. He'd been grinning at me this entire time, his smile charming.

All I could think about was Hunt.

Thorn's smile slowly faded away as he watched my stoic expression. It kept disappearing until it was completely gone, his face just as hard as I was. The car vibrated slightly as we headed to the event, the businesses along the sidewalk all lit up. Classical music played in the background, but the car felt silent. "Titan?"

"Sorry...I just wasn't expecting you to say that."

"You're thirty, so I know you've got a timer on your eggs. It's the perfect timing. We'll be married for a year, and then we'll pop out our first kid. We probably shouldn't wait much longer anyway. You have any idea how cute our kids will be?"

"Yeah..."

"So that night is good for you?"

"Uh..." I couldn't get Hunt's face out of my head. Just the other day, he'd said he didn't see us walking away from each other when his time was up. I didn't say anything at the time because I didn't know what to say. And now I would tell him I was getting engaged to Thorn... He wouldn't take that well.

Thorn dug into his pocket until he found the small box. "I know you're simple and don't want anything too flashy. But since you're going to be a Cutler, I had to go all out." He opened the black box and revealed a white-gold band with a solitaire diamond. But the diamond was huge. I'd be worried about knocking it on things all the time. "Or Titan-Cutler. Whatever you want."

I watched the diamond reflect the light, casting rainbows inside the car.

"What do you think?"

"It's beautiful..." I couldn't pull the words out of my brain because I didn't know what to say. It truly was extraordinary.

"It took a lot of searching for me to find it. But it was worth the wait."

I stared at it, speechless.

Thorn finally closed the box and stuffed it into his pocket. "Is it okay? Because there's still time to get something else. I haven't shown it to anyone."

"No...it's perfect."

"Great." His smile was back on his face.

I faced forward and looked out the window, feeling the car shift when it turned left at the light. I gripped the door handle as I looked outside, seeing the lights blur as we moved. A million thoughts were going through my mind, each of them heavier than the previous one. "What made you decide to do this now?"

He shrugged. "Why wait?"

Thorn and I had never picked a date. We just assumed it was somewhere in the future. When it was the perfect time for both of our professional lives, we would tie the knot. Nothing had changed much in our careers, but he obviously thought otherwise. "Especially with that shoot you did with Connor, your popularity will be through the roof. Stocks will rise, and we'll both benefit. I think now is the best time."

Maybe. Maybe not. I wasn't sure.

"Titan?"

"Yeah?"

"Are you alright?"

"Yeah, I'm fine," I lied. "I just...that ring is huge."

He chuckled. "Yeah, it is. But only the best for my future wife."

Future wife. I was Thorn's future wife.

And Hunt's future memory.

7

HUNT

I WANTED to remove Thorn from this equation.

I was the one in charge, but he had a distinct hold over her. I didn't have a clue what the man did to deserve her unflinching loyalty, but he never should have been the recipient of it. If he really cared about her, he wouldn't engage in this false relationship. He wouldn't allow her to marry someone she didn't really love.

He was the one benefiting from this relationship a lot more than she was.

Why didn't Titan see that?

I stayed at home that night and watched the game, ignoring people's texts when they asked if I was at the gala that evening. My mind kept circling back to one of the last things I said to her. I took her face in my hands and said we weren't going to walk away from each other.

That when this arrangement ended, a new relationship would begin.

She never corrected me.

Disagreed with me.

Said anything at all.

That told me there was hope.

That I wouldn't be another name on her list.

That I would be something more.

When ten o'clock rolled around and I didn't hear from her, I texted her. *Where are you?*

The three little dots popped up. *I just got home. I'm not feeling well, so I'm going to turn in for the night.*

I leaned forward on the couch, my elbows resting on my knees. *What's wrong?*

Not sure. Just an upset stomach.

Something told me she was lying, but I had no idea why. The context of a text message was hard to decipher. She might be lying to avoid the punishment she was due, but a fearless woman like Titan wasn't scared of anything. *How can you have an upset stomach if you don't eat anything?*

I guess I drank too much.

If she drank too much, she'd be begging me to come over. *I'm coming over.*

Why? I could actually hear her demand in the word.

Because I know you're lying to me.

When I didn't get a response from her, I knew I was right.

I WALKED INTO HER PENTHOUSE AND NOTICED THE EMPTY glass on the coffee table. There were still two ice cubes inside, so I knew she'd been drinking. Her lie was even more apparent now. "Baby, it's me." I walked down the hallway, making my presence known so she wouldn't be startled.

I found her in her bedroom, sitting on one of her couches in the gray shirt I gave her. A tablet was in her hand as she scrolled through the news. Her hair was a loose curtain around her face, and her makeup was still heavy because she hadn't removed it.

I sat beside her and rested my arm over the back of the couch. My arm pressed against her delicate shoulders, feeling their petiteness through the fabric. I watched her expression, noting how it didn't change when I walked into the room.

It always changed when I walked into the room.

"What is it?" My hand moved into her hair and tucked the strands behind her ear.

She didn't move at the touch. "I don't want to talk about it, Diesel."

"Why not? This is me we're talking about."

She finally looked at me, her eyes softening against their will. "I know…"

"You can tell me anything." I eyed her lips, seeing their plump smoothness. They were still vibrant red, but the color was smeared in places, probably from drinking from a glass all night. "I'll always keep your secrets."

"It's a secret I'm just not ready to tell. Nothing personal."

"Will you tell Thorn about it?"

Her eyes shifted away, and she looked out the window. "No."

Then it really wasn't personal. "I'm here when you change your mind."

"I know, Diesel. You're always there…"

I tugged on the collar of her shirt and kissed her shoulder, swiping my tongue across her skin. She seemed to feel better when my mouth was on her, when she was the recipient of my hot and carnal kisses.

She closed her eyes and released a hum so quiet, I wasn't sure if I heard it.

My mouth moved to her ear and kissed the shell. "Can I give you some advice?"

"How can you give me advice when you don't know what my problem is?"

"Because all problems are different, but all solutions are exactly the same."

She stared at me, her lips slightly parted.

"Just do whatever the fuck makes you happy. You've worked too hard to feel anything less."

Her gaze dropped, and a small smile formed on her lips. "Do you take that same advice?"

I was screwing the most successful woman in the world for a reason. "Every day."

She chuckled before resting her head on my shoulder. She pulled her knees to her chest and cuddled into my side.

I brushed a kiss to her forehead. "You still want me to leave?"

"No...I never want you to leave."

Maybe she did have too much to drink tonight. "Then I won't."

I CRAWLED ON TOP OF HER, MY NAKED BODY RESTING ON hers as I spread her thighs with mine. We'd spent the last half hour making out on the couch, exploring each other on top of our clothes like teenagers at a kissing party. I moved her to the bed once she undid my pants.

"How do you want me, baby?" I liked her just like

this, underneath me with beautiful tits staring back at me. Her smooth skin was soft like a flower petal, and her fairness made the surface easier to bruise with my tough kisses.

"I thought you were the one in charge?"

"I am. And I want to make love to you the way you want me to." I kissed her on the mouth, my tongue parting her small lips and delving inside. I didn't want to fuck her, to grip her by the throat and slam my cock into her ass. I wanted gentle kisses, quiet breathing, and slow sex.

"I didn't think Diesel Hunt made love..."

"I didn't think Tatum Titan did either...but that's what we've been doing." I pressed my head into her and moved all the way until I was completely inside her. My arms pinned her behind the knees, and I spread her wide apart, wanting all the room I could get to rock into her.

She bit her bottom lip and moaned. Her long nails dug into my arms, and her nipples hardened.

I let my cock sit inside her for a moment, surrounded by the wet tightness that made me feel more like a man. My thickness stretched her tiny cunt apart, filling every single inch of space that her body could create. I made her feel full, giving her so much man that she felt just like a woman. "Baby...this pussy is all mine." I slowly thrust into her, feeling the slickness she produced just for me. I didn't believe she'd ever been so wet for another man, so tight. I didn't believe she'd ever enjoyed being with a man as much as she did with me.

"Yes..."

I held my face above hers and looked her straight in the eye as I slowly moved inside her, pushing deep and pulling out again. I kept my body rigid and tight, using my core to move in and out. Every time I was deep inside her, I never wanted to pull out.

I never wanted to leave.

"I'm already going to come..." Her hands wrapped around my wrists, and she used them as an anchor to slowly lift herself up and take my length.

"Because I always make my woman come."

"God, Diesel..." Her head rolled back.

"You love it when I call you that."

She bit her bottom lip again, tightening around me.

"Tell me."

"I love it when you call me that..."

"Tell me you're my woman."

"I am, Diesel."

"And I'm your man."

"Yes...you're my man." Her hand suddenly tightened further on my wrists, and she came, her face contorting into an expression of pure pleasure. "Yes...Diesel." She bit her bottom lip and thrust her hips upward, getting more of my length.

I wanted to come the moment she said I was her man. I buried myself deep inside her and released with a groan, pumping all of my white come deep inside her. I shoved it deeper, thrusting so it would stay inside her as long as possible. I wanted her to walk around all day with my seed sitting inside her, heavy and warm.

Because she was my woman.

Her hands ran up my chest, and she panted as she caught her breath. "More..."

My cock was softening, but it would only take minutes before it was back to full mast. "Yes, baby."

We didn't shower after sex like usual. We kept going at it until we were both satisfied. Then we rolled over and fell asleep. My limbs were wrapped around her even though I was hot and sweaty. The heat was fine as long as I got to be near her.

And she was all over me.

She clung to me like a little girl who needed her teddy bear to sleep well. When I looked at her, I saw the powerful woman who owned an empire. But after seeing that picture in the back of her father's book, I couldn't stop looking at her in an innocent way. She was just like everyone else, a vulnerable woman with feelings and sensitivities. She just erected skyscrapers and corporations around it.

I liked both versions of her.

But I'd always preferred Tatum.

I was dead asleep when I felt her shift in my arms. She didn't just turn over like she normally did in sleep. She was thrashing, her arms moving from left to right and her legs kicking.

I was partially conscious of what was happening.

But when she screamed, I was wide awake.

Tears were all over her face, and she struggled to breathe. Her hands were around her neck like she was choking herself.

"What the fuck?" I grabbed her hands and yanked them down.

She punched me so hard, I actually fell back.

She kept thrashing until she fell off the bed and hit the hardwood floor.

"Tatum!" I jumped over the bed and landed on the ground beside her.

Her eyes were open, and she looked at me like I was the one who had just been choking her. "Get away from me." Her voice was eerily calm, nothing like it was just a second ago. She scooted back on the floor, inching away from me. "Don't touch me."

I raised both hands in the air and stepped back.

She didn't turn her back to me as she kept scooting backward. She slowly moved, not blinking as her eyes stayed on me. When she thought there was enough distance between us, she finally stood up and walked into the bathroom. The lock clicked when she pressed it.

What just happened?

That wasn't a nightmare. That was a night terror.

I suddenly understood why she didn't sleep with anyone. The night terrors must be a regular occurrence for her. They were terrifying, disturbing, and frankly, dangerous. She didn't seem to recognize me, and if she'd had a weapon, who knows what she would have done.

I waited five minutes before I stood outside the bathroom door. "Baby...it's Diesel Hunt. I'm standing on the other side of the door. I'm not going to hurt you." Maybe she was sleepwalking. Maybe she still wasn't awake, still wasn't sure of her surroundings.

"Please leave, Hunt."

Now she was calling me by my last name again. "Baby, talk to me."

Her voice remained steady; Titan was the one in control. Her attitude was so calm, it was as if she was trying to convince me the outburst had never happened in the first place. "You should go."

"No. I should stay. This is where I belong —with you."

"I'm not going to unlock the door."

"Then I'll stay right here."

Silence.

I waited, hoping she would open the door.

"Hunt, please go. I'm not going to ask you again."

"You aren't going to hurt me." Maybe she wasn't afraid of what I would do to her, but the other way around.

"I just need to be alone right now."

"No one in the history of time has ever said that and meant it."

"Hunt..."

"We're in this together, baby. You can tell me anything. That applies right now."

Silence.

Why wouldn't she open up to me? I couldn't unsee the distress I just saw. I couldn't pretend I didn't see her choke herself. I couldn't pretend I didn't see a version of Tatum Titan I couldn't forget.

"I'm not unlocking that door," she whispered. "I need to be alone right now, Hunt. We can talk about this later...but not right now. Right now, I just need to... I need some space."

Listening to the heartbreak in her voice shattered my emotions. It hurt to hear her sadness. It broke me to listen to her pain. It was devastating that I couldn't help her, that she wouldn't allow me to.

"Please."

I knew she wasn't going to open the door for me. I knew there wouldn't be any progress made tonight. I knew I need to give her space. "Okay, I'll leave. But we are going to talk about this, Tatum." I wasn't going to sweep it under the rug and pretend it never happened. I wasn't going to let this slide, not like the other times she'd dodged my questions.

After a long silence, she responded. "I know."

I didn't get anything done because all I'd been thinking about was Titan.

How was she doing?

Did she go to work? She said she never missed a day, that she didn't get sick or take vacations. Would this qualify as an exception?

I went to Stratosphere at midday, the usual time we met and discussed our goals for the week. The assistants were working on the main floor, and I noticed Titan's door was wide open.

That meant she was there.

I walked inside without announcing my presence and walked straight to the desk.

She was perfectly groomed like always, sky-high heels, a tight dress, and perfectly manicured hair. Her makeup was done with the same detail as usual, and she looked as though she'd slept like a rock.

She looked up and met my gaze. "Good morning."

It was a shitty morning. I didn't go to sleep when I got back home last night. I sat in front of the TV and drank all night.

"I took care of some reports." She opened her drawer and pushed a stack of folders toward me. "I spoke with our product team in France. Everything is good on that end. I also hired a new marketing specialist. Didn't make sense to keep the previous guy..."

I didn't even glance at the folders. "Are we going to—"

"Not here, Hunt."

"Then when?" I wanted to growl like a pissed-off bear.

"I don't know...in a few days."

"In a few days?" I asked incredulously. "I don't think so. Tonight. My place or yours?"

"Hunt—"

"Diesel. Don't fucking call me that again."

She retained her composure even though I was practically yelling in her face. "I'm not ready."

"Don't give a damn. I gave you space last night. That's all you're getting from me. And if you ask me, that was pretty fucking generous."

"I don't appreciate your tone, Diesel." She warned me with the fiery look in her eyes.

"I don't appreciate your secrets, Tatum. You never answered me, my place or yours?" I thought she might not want to have the discussion where she had her freak out. Maybe the place was tainted to her now.

She didn't break eye contact with me, but her eyes wavered back and forth. "Yours."

I left her office without looking back.

———

TIME SEEMED TO TRAVEL SO SLOWLY AS I SAT THERE ON the couch. My glass sat in front of me, but it kept getting empty because I wouldn't stop drinking it. My decanter of scotch constantly kept refilling it, the ice cubes continually getting smaller and smaller.

Where was she?

Finally, the lights above the elevator lit up.

She was on her way.

I rose to my feet and stood in the entryway, ready to greet her the second she walked inside. I wouldn't bombard her with a million questions. She was there to talk. My job was to listen.

The doors opened, revealing Titan in dark jeans and a black t-shirt. It was an outfit I'd never seen her wear out of the house. She was casual, real. She obviously didn't care about making an impression tonight.

Which meant she was vulnerable.

Tatum was here.

I suddenly felt like a jerk for being so harsh with her earlier. I couldn't contain my frustration very well, annoyed I wasn't getting my way. My motivation came from a good place, but that didn't excuse my roughness.

I pulled her into my body and wrapped my arms around her, cocooning her from everything that haunted her. I was a man made of flesh and bone, but I had the power to protect her from everything—if she would just let me.

My lips brushed across her hairline, and I squeezed her into my chest, being the crutch she would never allow herself to have. I closed my eyes as I held her, and a second later, I felt her grip me with the same intensity.

I was grateful just to hold her, to finally be allowed to touch her. This was how I'd wanted to hold her last night, to cradle her like a child that just needed to feel safe. If she'd only unlocked that door, I could have fixed her.

Even though I'd never fixed anyone before.

Minutes passed until we'd been standing there for half an hour. I wanted to pressure her, to get the answers I was so anxious to hear.

But I had to be patient.

I finally pulled away and looked down into her face. She wore her Titan expression but with her Tatum eyes. She retained her strong posture but her vulnerable aura. While there were still walls erected around her heart, there were far fewer than before. "Can I get you something to drink?"

"No, I'm okay."

"You wanna sit down?" I guided her to the couch, the best place to have this conversation.

She sat beside me, her purse falling to the floor. She crossed her legs and kept her back perfectly straight. Even when she was at her weakest, she held herself with such strength. She looked at the floor for several heartbeats before she looked at me.

I held my tongue, letting her start whenever she was ready.

"I... Now you must know why I don't like to sleep with anyone."

"Yeah...I pieced that together."

"I have bad nightmares. Sometimes they happen a lot, and other times, they seem to go away."

A hundred questions popped into my head, but I didn't voice a single one.

"It's been going on for a long time, about ten years. I'm sorry that I startled you. I know what you saw, and... I'm just sorry."

"Don't apologize to me," I whispered. "You don't owe me one." Her remorse stemmed from her perfection. She'd let someone see an ugly side of her, a side we all had. There was no need for an apology.

"I'm sorry anyway," she whispered. "I'm sorry I didn't open the door...I just couldn't."

I rested my elbows on my knees and leaned forward, waiting for the heavy stuff.

"It all happened ten years ago...when I met that boyfriend you've asked me about a few times."

I knew that asshole had something to do with her coldness.

"Everything was normal when we met. We fell in love, moved in together, my business started taking off. He became really jealous and possessive. He got overtaken by greed. He wanted my money, but he didn't like my power. He didn't like the fact that I always excelled at everything I put my mind to, that I was more successful than he was. My success only reminded him of his failures. And that jealousy became more bitter and more hateful..."

I watched her lips move as she spoke.

"The relationship turned abusive at one point. I won't go into the specifics because they don't matter anyway. But he hurt me. And he would hurt me a lot." Titan talked like she was in the middle of a meeting, like what she said had absolutely no effect on her. She had a hard shell that couldn't be penetrated. "I contacted the police many times, filed restraining orders. The judge never considered my evidence sufficient enough, saying my bruises could have been self-inflicted. I was a just a woman with a sob story looking for sympathy. Every time I went to the police, he would only hurt me more. He would choke me until I passed out. The times he preferred to do it was when I was asleep..."

Fuck, I wanted to throw up.

I'd never been so angry and nauseated at the same time.

Titan had reached out for help, but the police turned her away. She wasn't safe in her own home, being choked every time she shut her eyes. It made me so sick I felt a different emotion I hadn't felt in a long time.

I wanted to cry.

"Thorn tried to help me in whatever way he could. I'd stay at his place a lot. He would protect me, place his body in front of mine anytime Jeremy came near me. But Thorn had a job, and he couldn't be with me all the time..."

Now I felt like an asshole for ever hating Thorn.

"So Jeremy attacked me one day in my apartment. But this time, it was different. This time, he wasn't going to let me walk away with a few bruises..."

My eyes shifted to hers, needing to hear the end of this story.

"Thorn came in just in time and...killed Jeremy. He was the one who stabbed him in the heart. We both panicked and covered it up, making it look like someone broke in to the apartment and tried to rob us."

I played out the story in my mind, picturing Thorn stabbing a faceless man and letting him die on her kitchen floor. I pictured Titan's tears as she watched the blood spill everywhere. I imagined her remorse as well as her grief.

"The police never suspected otherwise. But I've always hidden that story away from the media because I'm afraid the world will dig a little harder...look a little deeper. They'll look over the evidence again, see the restraining orders I filed...and figure out there was no burglar at all. That I killed him. Or worse, that Thorn was the one who did it."

Now everything made sense. I understood why she was so restrained from sharing that piece of history with me. It was incriminating to her closest friend, the person who'd protected her when no one else did. Despite my jealousy, I actually liked Thorn.

He was a good man.

I wanted to say something to make Titan feel better, but I was in shock. I didn't realize her past was so deeply disturbing...so painful. "I hope you don't feel bad for him. That asshole deserved to die."

"No. I never feel bad about it."

I looked at her, seeing the sincerity in her eyes.

"But I've never gotten over that feeling..." Her hands moved to her neck. "Of air being taken away from you. Of your lungs working to suck air down your windpipe, but two hands are obstructing your throat. I wish I would just get over it and move on, but I can't. The idea of sleeping with someone in the same room terrifies me. It's not that I think they're going to hurt me. It's just...it's instinct."

"No, it makes sense."

"When you and I started sleeping together, I was so scared. But then the nightmares didn't come. I slept well.

I thought that horrifying part of my life was over. But I guess it'll never be over."

"It will," I said with certainty. "You just need more time."

"Yeah...maybe."

I grabbed her hand and squeezed it. "Thank you for telling me."

"I've never told anyone else before...except Isa and Pilar."

Now I felt even more special, knew this was anything but a fling between us. Whatever we had was real, it was true. I tugged her into my chest and positioned her on my lap. Sometimes I forgot how small she was because she projected a presence three times as imposing. I rested my face against her cheek and held her there, giving her all the comfort I had. I had a few questions I was anxious to ask, but I was sure she didn't want to answer them.

"It's a part of my life I just want to forget about. Even if people didn't suspect I had something to do with his death, if people knew I had been in an abusive relationship...they would think I was weak."

"How do you figure that?"

"Because I was in the relationship at all."

"But you tried to get out of it." Titan shouldn't have to feel ashamed for a bad relationship she had over ten years ago. She was young at the time, didn't have a single family member to turn to. "If anyone actually thought less of you, they'd be completely insensitive."

"Well...that's how the world works. The higher your reputation, the further you have to fall."

"I understand why you don't want anyone to know, but I don't think anyone would think less of you. I certainly don't."

"Really?" She turned her face toward me more, her eyes now looking into mine.

"Never." I kissed the corner of her mouth as my arms tightened around her. I hugged her like letting her go wasn't an option. Feeling her breathe beside me, her frame still strong and unbreakable, comforted me. She'd been beaten and hit, and I needed to know she was okay, that those bruises didn't exist somewhere deep...under the skin. I wasn't the one who had experienced such a horrible trauma, but I felt like the recipient of it. The idea of someone hurting Titan made me sick to my stomach. It made me want to murder a man who'd already been dead for ten years. "I still think you're the strongest woman in the world...and I admire you."

THORN HAD A BUILDING HERE IN MANHATTAN, ONE OF HIS

side businesses he ran. His tomato company was based in Chicago, but he had factories all over the country. He was a smart man and reinvested his profits into other companies. Now, he spent most of the time here—alongside Titan.

I checked in with his assistant then waited to see him. If this were anyone else, I wouldn't be waiting in that lobby. No one ever made me wait. If Diesel Hunt ever stopped by, you took the meeting instantly. You stopped what you were doing, knowing my presence was something of a gift.

But Thorn made me wait.

No doubt, on purpose.

He stopped by my office like he'd been entitled to the visit, and now I was returning the favor.

His assistant finally led me into his gray office. He had black furniture and a black desk, his tastes similar to mine. There wasn't a single item that countered his aura of masculinity. There wasn't even a picture on the wall. He sat behind his desk, leaning back against his chair with his dangerous eyes on me. He looked affronted even though I hadn't said a single word to him.

I took a seat, ignoring his hostility because my hatred for this man had ceased overnight. Every bad feeling I had toward him no longer seemed to matter. He won my loyalty and my respect the second Titan told me what he had done for her.

"Can I help you?" Thorn asked coldly. "If you're here to discuss my future wife, a phone call would have sufficed."

Hearing him refer to her so possessively didn't even bother me. Not right now. "It is about her...but I needed to say this to your face." I gripped the armrests as I sat in the tall chair, my legs crossed and my suit button undone.

His eyebrows arched.

"She told me what happened with Jeremy."

Thorn stiffened in his chair, and his eyes narrowed in a menacing way. He looked like he wanted to stab me in the eye with his pen. "What did I tell you about that?"

"I didn't ask her."

"You expect me to believe she just told you?"

"She had a nightmare a few nights ago...so she explained where it came from."

Thorn's anger dimmed, but only a tiny bit.

"She told me he was abusive and he wouldn't leave. And you were the one who protected her...and you were the one who killed him."

Thorn didn't confirm it, but he didn't deny it either. He dropped one elbow on the armrest and placed his knuckles under his chin. He kept up his poker face, hiding every single thought from my knowledge.

"I came here to thank you."

"Thank me?" he whispered.

"Yeah. You were there for her, you looked after her, you did the right thing...I would have killed that bastard too."

He lowered his hand and returned it to the armrest. The ferocity in his gaze softened as he slightly cocked his head.

"I apologize for giving you shit all the time. If I'd known you'd done that for her...I wouldn't have said a single word. You deserve my respect, so now I'm giving it to you."

His expression softened even more until I was looking at a different version of Thorn. He wasn't the ferocious competitor that didn't deserve Titan. He was just a man, a human being. His suit and office no longer mattered. His wealth and reputation didn't matter either. Now we were just two men who cared about the same woman.

"I just wanted to thank you for what you did. I'll go now." I rose from the chair and buttoned the front of my suit.

"I don't know what to say, Hunt. I'm surprised she told you...and I'm more surprised that you're standing in front of me right now. You're thanking me for something I did before you even knew her."

"She's a good person. She deserves to have someone look out for her the way you did." I didn't want Titan to marry Thorn, but in the end, he was a good candidate. He was loyal and protective. When it came down to choosing a partner, she couldn't find someone more committed.

"I'm glad you've finally come around."

"I believe you earned my respect. That's all I'm saying."

"Even so, I'm glad you're handling this so well."

"Handling what so well?"

"That you lost."

I hadn't lost anything. When our three weeks were over, everything would be different. I was even more confident than I had been before. Now that Titan saw me as one of her closest friends, Thorn didn't have much over me. "I haven't lost anything, Thorn. I still have time."

He examined me with suspicious eyes, his brain working furiously. His eyes shifted back and forth slightly, and then a slow smile crept onto his lips.

"What?"

He sat up straighter but didn't hide his grin. "Nothing." He came around the desk and extended his hand.

"Since Titan is the woman connecting us, I don't mind moving forward in a new direction. Perhaps we could be associates. And maybe someday...even friends."

I knew there was something more behind that smile. He knew something, but he refused to share it with me. Unlike with Titan, I wouldn't be able to pull it out of him with excessive questions. Thorn didn't owe me anything.

I didn't want to shake his hand, but I knew he deserved the gesture. I took his hand, and we both shook hard, gripping each other's hand with iron-hard clasps.

He looked me in the eye and nodded. "For what it's worth, I think you're a pretty good guy, Diesel Hunt."

"And for what it's worth, I think the same of you."

8

TITAN

As soon as I walked in the door, Thorn called me.

"Hey, what's up?" I slipped off my heels as I sat on the couch. The five-inch stilettos were pointed at the ends, where they squished my toes together. I never cared about the discomfort because they looked amazing with every outfit I wore. They were fairly comfortable, as comfortable as they could be for a shoe like this.

"Your boy toy stopped by my office today."

"He did?" I massaged the bottom of my foot, but I was only half paying attention to what I was doing. "Why? What did he say?"

"He told me you told him about Jeremy."

That was the first thing he did after I told him my secret? Ran off and opened his mouth? "What else did he say?" Why would Hunt tell Thorn about all of that when Thorn obviously knew the story—he was there.

"Said he wanted to thank me for protecting you."

I stopped rubbing my foot and sat back into the couch, suddenly breathless. Hunt and Thorn were always hostile to each other. I couldn't picture Hunt going out of his way to be even remotely nice to Thorn.

"And he said he respected me for doing the right thing...for killing that asshole."

I still didn't know what to say. I was touched that Hunt went over there and thanked Thorn for what he did. He dropped all of his jealousy to say something nice. That was impressive for a stubborn man like him. And one who was psychotically jealous. "I'm surprised he did that."

"I've always known he was a good guy. Most men are crooks or perverts. Diesel Hunt isn't one of them. He stands on his own two feet, protects those who can't protect themselves, and he truly admires you. I don't have anything bad to say about him...but that doesn't mean I like him."

"You know that makes no sense, right?"

"He wants to keep you to himself. How am I supposed to like him?"

I didn't correct Thorn this time. There was no way I

could do it without lying. And I didn't lie to my best friend.

"You didn't tell him about our engagement."

No, I didn't. And yes, it was on purpose.

"Why?"

"I just...haven't."

"I kept your secret. Figured you'd want him to hear it from you instead of me."

"Thank you."

"I guess there's no harm in waiting to tell him until your arrangement is over. Three weeks, right?"

Hunt must have told him that. "Yeah."

"Let the guy down easy. He genuinely cares about you."

"I know he does..." I could feel it every time he looked at me, every time he touched me. I laid my heart open to him, and he accepted my story without judgment. He said he admired me for everything I'd been through. He was a good man, one of the best I'd ever known.

"I know you care about him too. And I'll be there for you when the time comes."

―――――

HUNT SUMMONED ME TO HIS PENTHOUSE AFTER DINNER.

He sent me a simple message since he was a man of few words. *Get over here.* He was back to his bossy ways, commanding me like a general.

I was dropped off at his place, this time, a bag over my shoulder. I suspected he wanted me to spend the night despite my own reservations about it. He wouldn't pity me for long. He was the kind of guy that believed in tough love.

I walked into his living room and saw him standing there to greet me.

He was shirtless and barefoot, only his sweatpants on his waist. They hung low on his hips, showing his eight-pack and the rest of the muscles he was packing. He walked up to me and lowered his face to mine. He gave me a soft kiss on the lips and gripped my hips. He pulled me into his chest and pressed our foreheads together. "Hey."

"Hey…" I was light-headed and weak-kneed. My breath was fast and shallow. I suddenly wasn't thinking about anything, my mind wiped completely clean. All I did was exist, listen to his heavy breathing and feel my heartbeat.

It was peaceful.

He pressed a kiss to my forehead before he released me. "How are you?"

"Good. You?"

"Had a long day and a long workout."

My hand explored his arm, feeling his thick biceps. "Thorn told me you stopped by today."

He was a foot taller than me, so he had to look down to meet my eyes. "Yeah."

"He told me what you said."

"I figured he would."

I stared at his arm again, unsure what to say. I thought I had to address his visit with Thorn even though there wasn't anything to talk about. It needed to be mentioned.

"Thorn is a good man. I'm glad you have him."

"He is..."

"I'll make a stronger effort to get along with him."

"He said you were a good man and he doesn't have anything bad to say about you...that you aren't like the other crooks out there."

"I'm sure he's always known that."

"Yeah."

"I feel like I owe him something."

"Why?" I whispered.

"Because if he hadn't done that, I wouldn't have you now."

I looked up at him, my eyes soft.

"You changed my life, Titan. In many good ways."

"I don't know about that..."

His hands cupped my cheeks, and he pressed his face close to mine. "Yes, you do. You brought me to life. I was dead inside...not feeling anything. But you make me a stronger man, you make me a more compassionate man."

"Diesel...you were perfect before I came along."

"That's not true, and we both know it." He kissed me on the mouth, his embrace tender and soft.

Now I'd never been more confused in my life. My heart pounded every time he touched me, and I felt so many sensations I'd never known. It was difficult to picture my life without him, to let him walk away and be with someone else. Even after my nightmare, I still wanted him to be in my bed, sleeping beside me.

I didn't know if I could let him go.

And he wouldn't let me go either.

Hunt scooped me up into his arms and carried me into the bedroom. He laid me down, my head landing on a pillow, and he lay on top of me, his thick arms holding his weight over mine. He didn't remove my clothes, and he didn't kick away his sweatpants. I assumed we were getting down to business, but he obviously had other ideas.

My fingers touched his chin, feeling the thick stubble that was coming in. I looked into his eyes, seeing those dark irises that reminded me of melted chocolate.

He was warmth on a winter day, comfort in a difficult time.

He pulled my leg over his waist, making my dress ride up and exposing my panties. He held me against him that way, his hard cock right against the lace of my underwear. Despite his hardness, he didn't undress me and take me the way he usually did.

Instead, he just looked at me.

"What?" I whispered. My fingers trailed down his face to his lips. I ran my fingertips over the softness of his mouth, feeling the flesh that kissed me all over. His chiseled face was hard like his jaw. He had terrifying eyes that were beautiful in their own way. His dark hair matched his eyes perfectly. His tanned skin looked like it was kissed by the sun often even though he was indoors most of the time.

"You're beautiful." He rubbed his nose against mine. "I enjoy looking at you."

My hand glided up his neck and into his hair. "You can do whatever you want with me, but all you want to do is look at me?"

"It's fascinating," he said with a smile.

"I think you need to find a more exciting hobby."

"I already do—and it involves you." He ground against me gently, his thick length pressing right against my clit.

My thighs squeezed him automatically.

He stopped grinding against me, taking away the friction that drove me wild. "There's something I want to say to you."

"I'm listening."

He grew serious, his playfulness evaporating. "These arrangements you have…"

I should have known that was what he wanted to talk about.

"What exactly are you afraid of?"

"What do you mean?"

"Why do you have arrangements instead of relationships? I know you aren't scared of anyone. You can take care of yourself. You have more power than most people combined. If anyone tried to lay a finger on you, that would be the last mistake they would ever make."

My fingers remained buried in his hair, feeling the soft strands as they curled around my fingertips. When I was underneath him this way, I had nowhere to go. I had to face his mocha eyes, his deep gaze. "That relationship with Jeremy was passionate. It wasn't always bad. The beginning was great. The conversations were deep, the sex was good. But that passion changed form. He turned possessive and jealous, but not in a healthy way. The more he felt me slip away, the more he grabbed on to me. It turned into a destructive and abusive relationship.

That experience made me realize that passionate love doesn't exist. There's only lust, desperation for power. And when it grows, it becomes dangerous. I decided then that I didn't want another relationship like that. I wanted friendship, love, trust, loyalty...true love. And that's exactly what I have with Thorn. We aren't in love. We aren't passionate toward each other. But there's so much respect that it's beautiful. It's comfortable. It's safe. Relationships like that are long and happy."

"And your arrangements? Your need for power?"

"It gives me what I'm missing with Thorn, the passion that I crave. But in these scenarios, the men don't have any power. They have no control. I'm the one in charge. There's no risk. I can fulfill my fantasies without risking my heart."

His expression didn't change as he listened to every word. "But you made an exception for me."

It wasn't a question, but I took it as one. "Yeah..."

"Because you trust me."

"At the time, I just wanted you. I was willing to do anything to have you."

"And now we have something far better than an arrangement. We have friendship, trust, loyalty, and respect. We have everything you've ever wanted—including passion." His eyes didn't blink as they looked into mine.

I stared back, feeling my heart ache and my body quiver. He'd cornered me into a tiny space where I couldn't run. His heavy body weighed me down, and he had me in the most intimate position possible—with unflinching eye contact.

"I know you feel the same way, baby."

"You do?" I whispered.

He nodded. "It's obvious."

"I don't know about that..."

"I do. You've given yourself to me—completely."

"When?"

"The second you put me in charge. You never would have done that unless you trusted me. You never would have let me sleep with you if you felt unsafe. You never would have made me your business partner if you suspected I was anything less than truthful. You haven't said any of those things to me, but you don't need to. You've shown me."

Maybe I was letting my heart make all the decisions for me. I was losing my logic, losing my critical thinking skills that got me to the top. I was letting my body and my hormones do all the thinking.

"I'm not like the others."

"No...you aren't."

He finally pulled my underwear down my thighs until they were gone from my ankles. He parted my legs and pulled his boxers and sweatpants down to his ass. He moved between my thighs and slid inside me.

I gripped his arms and moaned.

He moved completely inside and held his weight on both arms. He pressed his forehead to mine as he stretched me deep and wide. "I'm the only man you've allowed to make love to you."

As the day passed, I was sinking deeper into my own turmoil.

Hunt showed me his feelings, wearing them on display like a sandwich board. He didn't say anything to me directly, but his intentions were perfectly clear. To him, I really was his woman. There was no end to this arrangement.

Because there was no arrangement at all.

Thorn said I should wait to tell Hunt about my plans to become engaged to him, but the longer I waited, the more I was going to hurt Hunt.

I had to tell him.

It was the right thing to do, even though I really didn't want to do it.

But I respected him too much to let this continue.

When I finished work the next day, I was the one who texted him. *Come over.*

I'd love to. Want me to bring anything?

Just you.

That's all my woman ever needs.

He kept calling me that, and every time he did, it sent a chill down my spine.

He arrived at my penthouse fifteen minutes later. He was in jeans and a t-shirt, his jaw clean since he shaved as soon as he got home. He greeted me with a kiss and a tight pinch of my ass. "You want me now? Or later?"

"How about both?"

"Good answer." He chuckled against my mouth before he kissed me again. His nose brushed against mine, and he looked at me like I was the only thing in the world that mattered. I was the focal point of his universe, the sun that he circled every single day.

I loved it when he looked at me that way.

His hand cupped my cheek, and his eyes slowly fell as he looked into my face. His thumb brushed against the corner of my mouth before he lifted my chin, making my gaze angle higher to reach his eyes. "What's wrong?"

"What makes you think anything is wrong?"

"Because I know you, Tatum. You fool the rest of the world, but you don't fool me."

I was never trying to fool him—just myself.

"Talk to me."

I didn't know if we should sit down in the living room or lie down in the bedroom. Or maybe we should just stay here, standing in the living room while the TV was on in the corner. I'd never been nervous to talk to him before. My stomach was tied in my knots, and my knees weren't strong like they usually were. "Thorn and I did some talking and...he's going to propose in a few weeks."

"Propose to whom?" he asked, his eyebrows furrowed.

"Me..."

Hunt stared at me with the exact same expression, his eyes fixated in one spot. The reflection of the city lights could be seen on the surface of his pupils, soft and nearly invisible. His hand paused on my face, his pulse no longer detected. Time seemed to slow down for both of us as he soaked in my words and I forced myself to say them. "You still want to marry him?"

"That's what we agreed on."

Once he snapped out of the shock, he moved his hand to my neck. "You didn't answer my question."

"Yes...I guess."

"You guess?" He spoke with a clenched jaw, his

mouth so tight it was about to come unhinged. "That doesn't sound very convincing to me."

"I made a commitment to Thorn...and I keep my promises."

"What kind of man makes a woman promise to marry him when she's clearly in love with another guy?"

"I'm not in love—"

"Bullshit, Titan," he hissed. "You're really going to look me in the eye and say that to me?"

I shut my mouth, now my jaw just as tense as his.

"This isn't an arrangement anymore, Tatum. This is a relationship. I was never going to walk away in three weeks. And you're an idiot for thinking you were ever going to walk away either."

"I set out the rules of this arrangement...and I intend to keep them."

"Rules don't apply to us."

"They apply to everyone."

He dropped his hand, giving me a stare more livid than any other before. "You can't be serious right now."

"I told you my intentions with Thorn from the very beginning."

"No, actually. I had to pull that out of you like a dentist ripping out teeth."

"You still knew about it, Hunt—"

"Diesel. There's no switching back now."

I'd known he wouldn't take this well, but I didn't realize just how difficult it was going to be.

"You said you wanted a partner you can trust. You said you needed trust, friendship, loyalty, and respect."

"Yes. Thorn can give that to me."

"And so can I," he snapped. "And I can give you everything else."

"And that's the problem..."

"The problem?" he asked. "Don't pretend that you don't trust me because you do. There's no way you can walk away from this and be happy. I'd be miserable without you, Titan. And you sure as hell would be miserable without me."

I would.

"I'm done playing these games," he said. "I'm throwing my cards on the table. Tatum, I want to be with you. I don't want to go back to hooking up with nameless, meaningless women and pretending to be happy. I found the one woman who actually makes me feel something. I found a woman whom I admire and respect as my equal. I love everything about you. And I don't need to hear you say that back to know you feel the same way."

I stepped back, letting his hand slide off my cheek. "Hunt..."

"What?"

"This is exactly what I didn't want."

"Too fucking bad," he hissed. "It happened. I wasn't expecting it either."

I stepped back farther and crossed my arms over my chest.

He stared me down, his expansive chest rising and falling at a rapid rate. "I can give you everything he can."

"It's not about what you can offer me."

"Then what is it? Unless you're in love with him, which I know you aren't."

"I just...I owe him." That was the truth of the matter. It didn't matter how strongly I felt about Hunt. I was loyal to Thorn. He did more for me than anyone else in the world.

"What do you mean by that? Because he killed Jeremy? You don't owe him anything, Tatum. That asshole deserved to die. If Thorn is going to hold that over your head, then he's just as bad as Jeremy."

"He doesn't hold anything over my head..."

"Then how do you owe him?"

"He was my first investor. I was broke, without a penny to my name. I had no collateral, so I couldn't get a loan from the bank. He loaned me a hundred grand. Without him...I wouldn't be where I am today."

Hunt finally dropped his anger, understanding coming into his gaze.

"He has a lot to do with my success. So my earnings and my assets are all connected to him. Marrying him, even if it is just for convenience, benefits both of us."

"How did this even come up?"

"I said I never wanted to be in a relationship again... and Thorn said he couldn't marry anyone because they'd just be after his money."

"So this was a mutual agreement?" He walked to my bar and poured himself a glass of scotch.

"Yes."

"Then why was he so eager for us to be together? He was practically pushing me on you." He drank the entire glass like it was a shot then refilled it. He moved to the couch and sat down.

I slowly walked toward him before I took the seat beside him. "Thorn has always wanted me to move on from my control issues..."

"Why?"

"Because he..." I wasn't sure if I should tell this secret since it wasn't mine to tell.

"We're putting all our cards on the table now," Hunt said as he stirred his drink. "Everything needs to be out in the open."

I'd already told Hunt my darkest secret. Did it matter if I told another? "Thorn is like me...he likes to be in control in his own arrangements. He exposed me to the lifestyle once I was ready to be with men again."

"I guess that makes sense."

"But he's not willing to compromise in our relationship. He needs to be in control. And since I allowed you to control me...he hopes I'll do the same for him."

Hunt nearly shattered the glass he was holding. His veins bulged in his forearms.

"We haven't talked much about our sex life, but I—"

"I don't want to hear about it." Instead of breaking the glass, he took a long drink. "This man saved your life and built you from the ground up..." He shook his head and wiped his lips on the back of his hand. "I get it."

I watched him stare at my fireplace as he refused to look at me. He'd never brushed me off like this before, shutting me out. He wouldn't let me look into his eyes, the gateway to his thoughts. His muscular body was tensed, like a provoked bear that would strike at any moment.

I felt like shit.

He leaned forward and rested his elbows on his knees. His palms came together, and he rubbed them gently as he stared at the floor.

Now everything felt strained. Our comfortable and calm relationship was gone. Hunt had placed an invisible wall between us.

I wanted to say something to make this better, but I couldn't think of anything.

"Thorn cares about you." When Hunt spoke, the words almost didn't make sense. "If you told him you wanted to be with me, he would understand. He would want you to be happy. That's what real friends do." He finally looked at me. "And Tatum Titan doesn't do anything she doesn't want to do. So the question is... what do you want?"

I stared at his espresso eyes, then observed the power radiating from all of his extremities.

"Baby?"

"It's not about what I want..."

"Yes, it is."

"It's a lot more complicated than that. If I marry Thorn like I planned, my future is set. I know exactly what will happen and when it'll happen. It's safe."

"And fucking boring. I'm not a risk, Tatum."

"Yes, you are. Even if we wanted to have a relationship, we have no idea where it would go, how long it would last."

"That doesn't matter."

"It does matter. If I publicly break things off with Thorn, I can't go back to him. It would make him look bad."

"Who cares what the media thinks?"

"I do," I snapped. "The media has control of everything. It even affects the stocks in my companies. Being liked is more important than anything else. It opens doors."

He rubbed the back of his neck, growing visibly frustrated. "You'd rather settle for a fake relationship than be in a real one with a man like me?"

"It's not about what I would rather have…"

"Yes, it is, Tatum. You can't possibly do this."

"It makes the most sense. I can't jeopardize all of my plans because I've developed feelings for you."

"They aren't just feelings, Tatum."

I looked away, unwilling to meet his expression. Whenever I looked into those eyes, I couldn't hide myself from him.

"You're in love with me."

I took a deep breath at the words but still didn't look at him. I refused to acknowledge what he said. I refused to admit it.

"We both know it's true."

I kept my eyes focused straight ahead.

"So I don't believe you could marry Thorn and not think about me. I don't believe you could be his and not wonder where I'm sleeping at night. I don't think you could work with me every day and ignore the smell of women's perfume on my suit. It would eat you alive. I know how jealous you get."

"Just because I'd be married doesn't mean we can't continue this relationship. Fidelity is something that Thorn and I never promised each other."

"Are you serious right now?"

I turned back to him, seeing his hard expression.

"I'm not going to screw a married woman, even if Thorn is okay with it. That's not the kind of guy I am."

"Then I guess we'll stop when I get married."

"No. We'll stop the second you're wearing his ring."

Now that the ending of our relationship was even closer, I felt the panic creep into my veins. He was already slipping away, disappearing.

"I can see how much you don't want that. I see it in your eyes right now."

I blinked then shifted my gaze to the TV.

"I know you want to be with me." His voice turned gentle. "Take the risk, Tatum. I've more than proven myself to you."

"I know..."

He moved toward me and slowly lowered my body onto the couch. He climbed on top of me, covering my body with his massive size. His face hovered against mine, and he looked at me as if he had me cornered—a second time. "I know you told me how this was going to be. You set a deadline and rules. I expected to follow them... I never expected to feel this way. I never expected to fall for you."

I forgot to breathe as the words entered my heart.

"And now, I don't want to share you. Now, I want to rule this city with you. I don't want to move on with my life and leave you behind. I don't want to shake your hand and pretend to be your friend. It just happened... and I never meant for it to happen. But you need to understand I'm not like that asshole. I would never lay a hand on you, Tatum."

"I know that, Diesel... I never thought that."

"Then don't let the past ruin what you could have now. Don't pick Thorn just because he's the safe bet."

"I know..."

"You don't owe him anything. If you want to be with me, he'll step aside. I know he will."

Yeah, he probably would. He'd be disappointed, but not angry.

"Just think about it. I know this didn't fit into your plans. I know if it doesn't work out between us, you'd lose everything you built. But...I think it would be worth it. I want you so much now...and I doubt that'll ever change. The more I have you, the more I want you." He moved into me and kissed me on the mouth. "Please think about it. Just think about it." He kissed me again, his soft mouth making love to mine.

My lips automatically moved with his, my hands slipping into his hair. The passionate roar erupted in my heart, and I pulled him closer to me, swept away in his eager embrace. The clothes didn't come off, but that didn't stop us from wanting each other, from grinding against each other like there was nothing keeping us apart.

9

HUNT

I WAS ANGRY.

About everything.

I was angry that I let myself go soft for Tatum Titan. I was annoyed that Thorn was integral in her rise to success. I was pissed that this ex of hers made her question if real love existed.

And I was livid she didn't pick me.

There was still time—and lots of hope. Whether she would admit it or not, I knew how she felt about me.

And I only knew that because I felt the exact same way for her.

What we had was rare. It was true. It was something I'd never felt before—and I'd been with a lot of women. She and I had a connection that was stronger than blood. There was no way she could marry Thorn and let me go.

No way.

She caved to me in the first place, gave me the control in the relationship. She wouldn't do that for anybody—only me. I knew she would realize Thorn was the safe bet and I was a wild card—but she needed my passion.

She couldn't live without me.

She couldn't live without the sex, the quiet conversations in bed, the trust and friendship...and everything else we had. I was just as good a life partner as Thorn, but I was even better. I could give her what he couldn't.

I could give her everything.

I sat at my desk for an hour straight and got nothing done. I put my feet on the desk and looked out the window, staring at the shadows from the buildings as the sun progressed in its path across the sky. I never let anyone distract me from what I needed to get done, especially a woman, but Titan was the only thing on my mind.

Natalie's voice entered my office. "Sir, Brett Maxwell is here."

My brother had a bad habit of stopping by whenever he was in town showing off a car to someone. We usually got a beer when I left the office, but if he was only around for the early afternoon, he usually swung by. "Send him in." Even if I had a meeting, I usually pushed it back to accommodate him.

Because he was family—all I had left.

Brett walked inside, wearing a smile along with his beard. He was in a long-sleeved black shirt and dark denim jeans. He gave me a high five before he dropped into the chair facing my desk. "What's up, little bro?"

My feet were still on the desk. "Just taking in the sights."

"You look like you're being lazy to me."

I flipped him the bird.

He chuckled then put his own feet on the desk.

"You wanna die, big bro?"

"Just run me over with one of my cars. I'll die happy."

My smile immediately dropped.

It took Brett a moment to realize his insensitive comment. His eyes immediately fell, and he sighed through his teeth. "I'm sorry—"

"It's fine." I brushed it off, knowing he didn't mean to offend me. "What's new with you?"

"I just sold a car to a VIP."

"Who's this person?"

"Thomas Wade."

Wade was one of the most famous golfers on the planet. He had the endorsement of most companies. He had three TV commercials on the air right that moment. "How does he like it?"

"Fell in love the second he looked at it. Can't blame him."

"They are beautiful." I looked out the window again, the world beautiful making me think of a specific person.

"What's got you down?"

"What makes you think that?"

"Because you look like you haven't slept in three days."

No, I hadn't been sleeping. I was spending time away from Titan, giving her space to really think about her decision. I had enough confidence not to feel threatened by other men, but Thorn had bent over backward for her. Not only did he start her first business, but he actually murdered someone for her.

I couldn't top that.

"I just need a haircut."

"Bullshit. What's wrong?"

He would eventually ask about Titan, so I got right to the point. "I told Titan how I felt..."

"Didn't go well, I take it?"

"She says she's still committed to Thorn."

"Really?" he asked incredulously. "If she's been

fucking you for so long, the guy obviously doesn't satisfy her."

My brother hit the nail right on the bed. "I told her to think it over."

"I'm surprised you even gave her the option."

It was a testament to how much I liked her. The idea of going back to the bars and meeting random women to hook up with sounded unappealing. The sex was good, but they always overperformed, trying to be exactly what they thought I wanted. But with Titan, she did what she wanted. And when a woman knew exactly how she wanted a man to please her...that was the sexiest thing of all. "She's exceptional."

"I could have told you that. Hope it works out for you, man."

"Me too."

"I've never seen you like a girl...not even when we were kids."

I raised an eyebrow.

"You know what I mean."

No, I never showed romantic interest in anyone. Women were sex on legs. But with Titan, I didn't see her legs. I saw a powerful woman with a brilliant mind. I saw someone with a soft soul and a hard outer shell. I saw someone so deep that there was no bottom. I viewed her in a way I never saw anyone else. She wasn't just a beautiful woman I enjoyed pounding into the mattress. I saw her as a partner, as a friend, as someone who was such an innate part of who I was that I couldn't imagine my life without her.

"Want my advice?"

"No."

He grinned. "Keep fighting for her. War is just a series of battles. You have to win them all. And anyone will tell you that love is the biggest war we'll ever fight."

WHEN SHE DIDN'T INVITE ME OVER FOR A FEW DAYS, I knew she was taking my final message seriously.

She was thinking it over.

But spending every evening alone in front of the TV was getting lonely. I drank a lot, didn't eat much, and hit the gym a little harder. I did a lot of work from my laptop and lightened the load during the workday.

But nothing was powerful enough to distract me.

It made me fear what my life would be like if she picked Thorn.

It would be back to this.

I'd never minded my life before I met her. It was fulfilling at the time. But going from something spectacular to something so mediocre was...depressing. I finally gave in to my desire and texted her. *Miss you*. I'd never texted that to a woman in my life. It was something a pussy would say. But I sent the message the second the words were on the screen, no thinking twice about it. Tatum Titan made me into a man, but she also made me a romantic.

Her reply was instant. *Miss you too.*

Then invite me over.

You know you don't need an invite, Diesel.

That was the only invitation I needed. I left my penthouse behind and headed to her place a few blocks away. We both lived in Tribeca, the part of Manhattan with the wealthiest real estate. The streets were quiet, full of businesspeople with their families. I walked into her building and took the elevator to her penthouse. The doors opened and revealed the empty living room with the glow of the TV.

She stood there in my gray collared shirt, a sea of emotions on her face.

I stepped into the room and listened to the doors shut behind me.

Her face was impossible to decipher. She looked like she wanted to smile and cry at the exact same time. Suddenly, she ran to me and jumped into my chest, her legs wrapping around my waist as her arms hooked around my neck.

I caught her effortlessly, a smile forming on my lips. "You really did miss me."

She ground against me, her panties rubbing against the bulge in my jeans. "I think you missed me more."

My eyes darkened, and I carried her into the bedroom down the hall. "I've missed you every single day since I left."

"Then you must have been really uncomfortable." She smiled at me with her red lips, flirtatious and sexy.

"I relieved myself when necessary." I set her on the bed and tugged her panties down her long legs.

"Oh...that sounds sexy."

"Me beating off is sexy to you?" I pulled her shirt over her head before yanking mine off.

"Really sexy."

"And I was beating off to the thought of you."

She squeezed her thighs together and pulled her knees to her chest. "Ooh..."

Like I wasn't hard enough, she was driving me crazy. I pulled my jeans and boxers off and positioned myself at the foot of the bed, the same place where I fucked her in the ass for the first time. "Now you're going to get a live show." I slid inside her wet pussy, feeling her arousal surround me. She must have got wet the second I texted her and told her I was coming over.

"Diesel..." She was already into it, her head rolling back as she bit her bottom lip.

Good thing she wouldn't last long. I wasn't going to either. I pushed myself entirely inside her then leaned over her, looking down into the face that haunted me in my dreams. "You're beautiful when my cock is deep inside you."

"What about when it's not?"

"Still beautiful...just not quite as." I dug my hips deep and rocked deep inside her, wanting her to feel my entire length. I wanted to watch her lips quiver, listen to her moan, hear her beg me to fuck her harder.

Her hands locked around my wrists as usual, and she looked straight into my eyes, her mouth already gaping open. She moaned in tune with my thrusts, so loud and so sexy. She uttered my name every few seconds, enjoying me like she hadn't had me in years rather than days. "I missed your cock so much..."

"He missed you too, baby." I pumped into her, sliding through her increasing wetness.

Her nipples hardened like the tip of a knife, and a pink flush covered her chest. The color spread to her cheeks, giving her a sexy fire. "I'm gonna come, Diesel."

"I know."

"Harder."

I quickened my pace and shook the bed, hitting her

wooden headboard against the wall. The loud tapping matched the movement of my hips, getting in tune with the sexy moans she made. She screamed louder and louder, her nails biting me like they had teeth. When she hit her threshold, her head rolled back, her hips bucked upward, and she bit her bottom lip with the strength to draw blood. "Diesel...yes...yes."

I rocked her world, sending her to the moon and the stars. I rubbed her clit just to give her an extra push, a heightened experience to make her writhe underneath me. She already missed me, but I wanted her to know what she would be missing if she walked away from me.

Her moans and screams continued, slowly dissipating as the intensity trailed off.

I wanted to keep at it, but after this drought I'd been in, I wouldn't last. I shoved my entire length inside her and released, dumping all of my seed deep within her. The muscles of my chest tightened as the explosion ripped through me. It felt right being buried all the way inside her. It felt like home.

She grabbed my hips and pulled on me harder even though I already took up every inch of her body. "Yes..." She loved taking my come even more than I loved giving it. She was folded underneath me, her legs spread wide apart and a look of satisfaction on her face. She never looked so beautiful, thoroughly fucked and pleased.

I slowly pulled out of her and stared at her entrance. A buildup of my come was there, glistening against her swollen folds. I wanted to claim her like this every single day. I wanted Tatum Titan on my desk with her legs spread apart. I wanted every man in New York to resent me for having the most incredible woman in the world.

For fucking her every night.

We got into the shower when we were finished, our nightly routine that had been established long ago. I rubbed the soap into her body, enjoying the touch of her ultrasoft skin. Her petite shoulders were rounded and slender, her neck was elegant, and she had the most beautiful arch in her back. Her spine moved straight down, the muscles noticeable on either side of the divide. Her body was feminine and strong, and I loved gripping it with my hands.

The truth of our situation hung over both of our heads, but neither one of us mentioned it. There was nothing more to say about it. She'd have to make her decision on her own, not listen to me explain why picking Thorn was a mistake. Titan was logical to a fault. Every decision, no matter how personal it was, was a business decision. That was how she would treat this dilemma as well.

She scrubbed the shampoo into her hair then

turned around to rinse it out. She tilted her head back but moved her eyes to my face.

I gripped her tits, feeling the soap drip everywhere. She had the greatest rack, not too big and not too small. They were firm, round, and soft. My callused fingertips loved to feel the beautiful flesh in my hands. I could get off just from feeling her up like this.

She arched her back farther, her hands lathering the conditioner into her hair. "You're good with your hands."

"They just love your tits." I gave her a gentle squeeze before my hands trailed to her waist. "You have a beautiful body." My thumb moved over her belly button, feeling the small little slit.

"Thanks."

"Not eating really pays off."

"It does, doesn't it?" She tilted her head back and rinsed the conditioner from her hair.

I loved watching her in the shower. She looked sexy in her office, in one of my t-shirts, when she was riding me on the couch, but nothing compared to this. Her hair was molded to her scalp from the water, and her face was clean of any makeup. When she didn't have mascara or eyeliner on, her eyes looked smaller. But the fresh look made her appear naturally beautiful. She could go anywhere without a drop of makeup and men would still turn their heads just to glance at her.

We finished in the shower, dried off, and then headed to bed. Her hair was slightly damp because she didn't dry it all the way with a blow-dryer, but I liked the casual way her hair fell around her face. She picked up my shirt off the ground and pulled it on.

Would she still wear that if she chose Thorn?

We got into bed even though it wasn't even ten o'clock yet. I lay beside her, my arm hooked around her slender waist. I looked at her beautiful face, my chest loosening from the strings that constantly restricted it. Art brought peace to anyone who looked at it. That was exactly how I felt about the muse right in front of me. Just looking at her made me feel better, made me exist in a state of quiet.

She ran her hand up my chest, her fingertips drawing circles over my heart. She watched what her hands were doing, obviously not the least bit tired even though we were in bed together underneath her soft sheets.

"How have you been sleeping?" I wondered if my absence had affected her. I wondered if she had any more nightmares. I wondered if her life had been just as impacted by my absence as I was by hers.

"Haven't been sleeping much, honestly."

"Me neither." Most of my nights were spent alone. I slept in a king bed all by myself and never had had trouble falling asleep the second my head hit the pillow. But now that I was used to this sleeping companion, the silence of my bedroom frustrated me. I missed her quiet breathing, the way she made little sighs just as she fell asleep. She'd been in my life for a relatively short amount of time, but that span had more effect on me than any other experience. It seemed like she was always there...even though she wasn't. "That's why I'm here."

"So I can help you sleep?" she asked with a smile.

"Yeah. I thought I could do the same for you."

"It'll definitely help. I've reached out in the middle of the night to touch you a lot this week...and then I remember you aren't there."

My fingers tightened on her waist, feeling her pain because I felt it too. "I'm here now."

"I know..."

"And I can always be here...if that's what you want." I didn't want to talk about the painful situation between us, but it escaped my lips on its own. Titan would be risking a safe lifetime if she chose to be with me instead. She would mess up her plans, the time she wanted to start having children, everything she and Thorn had worked toward. It was a lot to ask, actually. I couldn't offer her any guarantees since the future was always unpredictable. But I could give a few things. "I'm loyal to you, Tatum. You already know that. I would never betray you. I would never lie to you. And I have your back—through and through."

Her hand moved up to my neck. "I know, Diesel. If I didn't, this would be a much easier decision to make." Her thumb brushed along my jaw, feeling the stubble from days' worth of not shaving.

My hand tightened around her wrist, and I brought her palm to my mouth for a kiss. I kissed her fingertips and her knuckles, wanting to worship this woman who had affected my life so deeply. I was asking her to take a risk for me, but I was taking a risk for her too.

I was willing to completely change my life—just for her.

10

TITAN

I WAS WORKING at my desk when Thorn stopped by for
a visit.

He entered my office and dropped into the chair
facing my desk. He got right to the point of his visit,
talking about business. We didn't officially share owner-
ship of any of our companies, but we still worked
together to make our assets as successful as possible. If
we were going to combine our holdings, we wanted to
bring as much to the table as we could.

Thorn scrolled through his phone as he ran off
numbers to me.

I recorded what he said then discussed Stratosphere.
It was a slow launch in the beginning, but Hunt and I
were seeing success immediately. Bruce Carol was arrogant, and he'd thought he could coast by doing the bare

minimum. That was his downfall—along with outright stupidity.

"So, what's new with you?" Once business was out of the way, Thorn got comfortable and regarded me with his ice-blue eyes. He cocked his head slightly, his aura of ruthlessness gone when it was just the two of us.

"Nothing."

"Nothing?" he asked incredulously. "There's not a single thing?"

"Well...I got a new rug for my living room."

"For being the richest woman in the world, I would expect you to have a more interesting lifestyle."

I used to feel that way, until I got stuck in this difficult position with Hunt. I'd never struggled to get out of my previous arrangements. The sex was great, but by the end, I was ready to move on. If the men wanted to stay, they never voiced their desires. Probably because they knew I would say no.

But now my future was murky. It had been lined up perfectly just weeks ago, but now there was no path. It was difficult to lead an interesting life when I was stuck at this fork in the road. I could stay with Thorn and miss Hunt. Or I could choose Hunt and be happy, but then regret it later.

Thorn was the person I went to for advice, but this time, I couldn't.

Thorn continued to stare at me, his gaze cold and piercing. He had a particular way of examining me, looking at me like he could see right through me. It was something about the way his eyebrows shifted forward. "Titan, I feel like you aren't telling me something. I know that's unlikely because you tell me everything... but it sure seems that way."

Yep, he could see right through me.

"What is it?" he pressed. "Remember you're talking to me."

"Well...this whole thing with Hunt is complicated."

"What whole thing?"

"I told him you and I were going to get engaged soon...and he told me not to do. He asked me to be with him instead."

Thorn's expression didn't change, blue and cold as ever. He was usually transparent with his thoughts, his expressions as easy to read as a book. He put his soul on display for me, having nothing to hide after everything we'd been through. "And?"

"I just...I'm confused."

"So, you want to be with him, then?" Thorn didn't love me. Never had and never would. What we had was stronger than that. If I didn't want to marry him, he certainly wouldn't take it personally.

"Yes...and no."

"Which is it?" he asked firmly.

"I want to be with him because...I don't want to lose him. I can't imagine us going our separate ways. I don't want to be with anyone else, and I certainly don't want him to be with anyone else. He makes me happy. I trust him. He's my friend...he's a good man."

"If you're afraid that I'm going to be upset with you, you don't need to worry about that. If that's what you want, you know I'll respect your decision. Will I be happy about it? No. Will I be disappointed? Hell yes. But that doesn't matter. This is about you, not me."

I was touched, and I felt stupid for ever suspecting Thorn would be anything but supportive. He'd been there for me through everything. We conquered the hard times just as we rejoiced during the good ones. "You're so good to me..."

"Because I love you," he said. "But you already knew that."

"Yeah...I did. After everything you've done for me, I feel terrible for going back on our decision."

"Sweetheart, I didn't do those things for you because I wanted something in return. I did them because I cared about you...because you're my friend. You don't owe me anything, Titan. I gave you your first loan, but you're the one who built the empire on your own. I had nothing to do with it. You took a hundred thousand dollars and converted it into billions. All you, sweetheart."

I rested my fingers against my mouth, covering my emotion as much as possible. A thin film of moisture formed in my eyes, but I discreetly blinked it away. I'd never been good at these touchy-feely kinds of moments.

"Be with him if that's what you want. You have my blessing, not that you need it." He finally smiled at me, reassuring me that everything was truly okay. "But we'll need to figure out how to sort everything out in the media. We'll have to have a mutual breakup so neither one of us looks bad. And you can't start publicly seeing him right away—that'll make you look coldhearted."

We were jumping ahead of the game here. "I haven't made my decision yet."

"You haven't?" he asked. "Seems like you have."

"I want to be with him...but I think you're still the better choice."

"Well, obviously," he said with a grin. "Come on, look at me."

I chuckled and rolled my eyes. "If I end things between us, be with Hunt, and it doesn't work out...I know I can't come back to you."

Thorn didn't disagree with that statement. "You're right."

"So...I'd be risking everything."

"You would."

"With me, you'd have stability, security, protection, acceptance, honesty, and not to mention, good sex. You could have all that stuff with him...but will it last? I don't think either of you knows the answer to that."

No, we certainly didn't. "What do you think I should do?"

"You know I can't answer that."

"I always come to you for advice."

"But this is a conflict of interest. And I don't know how you feel about this guy. If you're in love with him... you may not have a choice. Are you in love with the guy?"

I shifted my gaze down to my desk and deflected the question.

"If you aren't sure, you need to figure it out. The truth is, if you aren't going to be with me, Diesel Hunt is a great choice. He's wealthy, smart, good-looking, honest, and he's not a sexist asshole. He respects you, clearly adores you. He'd be a great partner to have, and he wouldn't sell your secrets. But since all of this is based on passion and love...two things you oppose...I don't know what will happen. You might have a fight one day, and everything goes to shit. You divide your assets, and everything you've worked for comes crashing down around you. I'm not going to lie to you, Titan. It is a risk. You have to figure out if he's worth that risk or not."

"But—"

"You know I can't answer that for you."

I'd always been a woman who could think for herself, seeing the path ahead when everyone else didn't know which route to take. I analyzed situations differently from most people, which led me to acquire the best deals. But all that lifetime experience couldn't help me now. My last relationship was a disaster that ended up in murder. I obviously wasn't the best judge of character when it came to romance.

"But I will say this." Thorn crossed his legs, resting one ankle on the opposite knee. "You don't need to be afraid of the past repeating itself. What happened with Jeremy would never happen with Hunt. He's the last guy in the world you need to be afraid of."

"You have a high opinion of him…"

"I've always known he's a good guy. I didn't like him because I was afraid this would happen…which it did. And now that it has, I have no reason left to dislike him. He took my woman away, but I can't blame you for falling for him. That guy would take a bullet for you as quickly as I would."

"How do you know that?"

He shrugged. "Just do. I mean, the guy walked away from a billion-dollar company just because the owner insulted you. He could have done the deal and pretended it never happened. But he didn't. He declared war because someone slighted you. If that's not protective, then I don't know what is."

I'd never forget what Hunt did. It touched my heart. Loyalty was important to me, and it was obviously important to him too. "True."

"I haven't told the reporters about my proposal, so no harm done."

"What about your mother?"

He shrugged. "I'll figure out how to let her down easily. Don't worry about that."

"Thanks..."

"How long do you need to think about it?"

"I'm not sure yet. I'm just as undecided today as I was a few days ago."

"It's like you're in a love triangle," he said with a chuckle.

There was nothing funny about this. "I said I would never fall for another guy...and here I am."

"Don't beat yourself up over it. We all have weaknesses."

"You don't."

"Well, I'm not the romance kind of guy. Never have been, and never will be. That's just how I'm wired."

"Lucky you."

He smiled. "This whole situation is pretty ironic. The real reason why I wanted to propose now instead of later is because of Hunt. I thought if I waited too long, your relationship might get serious. I thought if I rushed in and took you now, I'd eliminate that possibility." He shrugged. "Looks like I didn't move quickly enough."

"Thorn...I'm so sorry."

He raised his hand. "Don't be. I want to marry you for my own selfish reasons. So don't feel too bad for me."

My eyes fell as the guilt swarmed me.

"Take all the time you need to think about it." He stood up and buttoned the front of his navy suit. "Seriously, Titan. There are no hard feelings. If he's the guy you want to be with, our relationship won't change. We're still in this together—for the rest of our lives."

JESSICA KNOCKED ON THE DOOR BEFORE SHE STEPPED inside. "Titan, flowers came for you."

Flowers? "Thank you. You can set them on my desk."

She carried the glass vase to the corner, where my

old vase of peonies was dying. She swapped them out and took out the wilted flowers before she left.

I stared at the small vase of purple irises. It was the perfect size for my desk, and the flowers were a beautiful color. I wasn't sure who sent them to me because I didn't recall ordering any. My flowers were usually changed tomorrow, so whoever sent these to me knew it was time for a refresh.

I found the card on the side and opened it.

Baby,

I have a new arrangement in mind. See you at my place at 7.

-*Boss Man*-

I WALKED INTO HIS PENTHOUSE AT SEVEN ON THE DOT, NOT wanting to be early or late. I didn't know what he had in mind, but Hunt was always full of good ideas. He wouldn't be so wealthy if that beautiful head of his were only full of clouds.

I walked inside and found him sitting on the couch. He was reading a book, bare-chested and barefoot. He was only in his sweatpants, and that was my favorite way to see him. I loved the way he teased me with his muscular physique but hid the best part of his package inside his pants. He slid the bookmark in between the pages and stood up to greet me.

My eyes were on his, absorbed in those coffee-brown irises. I felt weak when I was with him, but it was in a good way. No one else had any effect on my confidence. When they tried to intimidate me, I just stood taller. I was always the tallest person in the room—even when I was the shortest. "Thank you for the flowers."

"I knew they would look nice on your desk. Irises are your favorite, right?"

My heart beat a little harder. "How did you know that...?"

"You have flowers everywhere, all different kinds. But I noticed you have irises more often than any other flower...so I took a guess."

"Well...you were right."

He moved closer into my body, his chiseled arms thick by his sides. He looked down at me with his short hair flat against his head. He'd obviously dried his hair with a towel the second he stepped out of the shower. No matter what he wore or how much effort he put into his hair, he was the sexiest man in Manhattan.

He leaned down and tilted his head sideways so he could kiss me. It was a warm embrace on the mouth, his hand sliding into my hair. His mouth moved with mine, sucking my bottom lip into his mouth before he released it. I got some of his tongue, some of his warm breath.

I was a goner.

He brushed his lips past mine before he pulled away, ending the embrace before I was ready for it to stop.

My hands moved to his chiseled stomach, and I felt his hard physique. His stomach was just as hard as his chest. He was a tall wall with lots of curves. Made of brick and concrete, he was stronger than a stone fireplace that stood the test of time. "So...what kind of pitch did you want to make?"

"I don't consider it to be a pitch...but a compromise."

"What kind of compromise is there?" I wasn't asking Hunt for something he couldn't give. I just couldn't decide how much risk I was willing to take. If I chose Thorn, maybe I'd forget about Hunt in time. But in the beginning, it would hurt. It would hurt a lot.

"Thorn is offering you more than I am. What if I offered you the same thing?"

"How is he offering more?" Hunt was already loyal and honest. I trusted him just as much as I trusted my best friend. There was nothing more he could do to change my mind. It all came down to what I was willing to sacrifice.

"He's offering you security. And I'm willing to give you the same thing."

I had no idea what he meant by that, so I kept staring at him. "What does mean, Hunt?"

"Marriage, kids, partnership...I'll give you all of it."

Now my heart was beating even harder, thumping against my ribcage. Even though my pulse quickened, I felt like I wasn't getting enough blood to my extremities, enough air to my lungs.

"By choosing me, you're risking the perfect business relationship. You trust Thorn to be your partner, to be your friend. You trust for it to last because your relationship isn't based on lust. Well, I can give that to you. I'll marry you, Titan. I'll have kids with you. I'll give you the exact same relationship he's willing to give you. You can trust me to be your partner in life, to stand by your side every single day and remain loyal to you. I'm very wealthy, and together, our holdings would be impressive. I'm just as good of a candidate as Thorn. But I'm better—because I can satisfy you. I can fulfill all your fantasies—and you can fulfill mine."

When Hunt said he had an arrangement, this wasn't what I was expecting. I thought he wanted to extend our time together, explore some new sexual realm. I had no idea he would even consider this. "I...I wasn't expecting you to say this."

"Well, now I'm saying it. What do you think?"

"What do I think?" I asked incredulously. "You just proposed to me."

"I didn't propose—I asked you to marry me."

"Isn't that the same thing?" I snapped.

"I don't have a ring. But I can get you any ring you could possibly want."

I stepped back and dragged my hands down my face. "I just...wow."

"Is the idea of marrying me that surprising to you?" he asked coldly.

"No...I just didn't think you'd ever make an offer like this. Are you really willing to sacrifice falling in love with someone and starting a family just to be with me?"

His eyes bored into mine as he stared me down. His arms remained by his sides, but they shook slightly, the muscles and tendons flexing automatically. It was an aggressive look, full of irritation and anger. "I've already fallen in love."

Silence.

My heart stopped.

I forgot to breathe.

He kept staring at me, not ashamed of the declaration he'd just made.

I held his look, but I felt my confidence slip away. I suddenly felt dwarfed by his size, swallowed by his power. I finally took a breath because I needed it to stay grounded. My knees were locked, and I was about to topple over. "Oh my god..."

"And I know you've fallen in love with me." He moved closer to me, his face pressed to mine. "Tell me."

"Diesel..."

"Tell me that you love me." He moved his hand to my neck, and he gently lifted my chin so I was looking him right in the eye. "I know you already do, baby. You may as well say it."

"How do you know...?"

"I can tell just by looking at you...watching you look at me." His thumb slid over my pulse, and he felt my frantic heart rate. His eyes scanned over my face, sometimes looking at my lips and sometimes looking into my eyes. He knew what was coming, but he was patient enough to keep waiting for it.

My chest rose and fell faster, and my eyes burned with an emotion I didn't know I had. Both of my hands gripped his wrist as his hand continued to hold my neck. This was a something I never wanted to happen, an outcome I never could have predicted. But now, we were both here, our hearts hanging out of our chests like open wounds. "I love you, Diesel Hunt. I love you so much that it scares me." The second I blinked, a tear from each eye streaked down my face.

His thumb caught one of my tears and wiped it away.

His expression didn't match mine, full of emotional turmoil. He smiled in his handsomely classic way, feeling victorious once he heard my confession. "Baby...you're so beautiful when you cry." He leaned in and kissed the other tear that stopped halfway down my cheek. He moved his mouth to mine as he kissed me, his hand sliding into my hair. He fisted it as he kissed me in front of the elevator, his other hand gripping the small of my back.

I fell into him completely, finally handing myself over to another person. I'd kept myself so rigid and tight for so long, stopping myself from ever letting anyone in besides Thorn. But now the dam had been broken. My feelings poured out, and I let his feelings pour in. I kissed him back and tasted my own tears on his tongue. Now I was more vulnerable than I'd ever been before, letting Hunt see me completely for the first time. I had nothing left to hide because he saw all of me.

He scooped me into his arms and carried me into his bedroom. Right now, that was the only place I wanted to be. I wanted to sink into his mattress, his heavy weight pressing into me. I wanted that mouth, that cock, those eyes... I wanted him to smother me.

He yanked off my clothes and dropped his sweatpants before he crawled on top of me. He didn't waste any time getting inside me. With a single thrust, he was buried between my legs, plunging his lust and love deep within me.

"Diesel..." I locked my ankles together around his waist with my arms around his neck. My fingers were digging into his short hair, pulling on the strands in my desperation to get a hold of him, take as much of him as I could.

"Baby..." He flattened me into the mattress, thrusting deep as he pushed his way inside me. He held his body only inches above mine, his thick arms supporting all of his massive weight. He ground himself inside me, rubbed his pelvic bone against my clit, and gave me the most seductive kisses. "Tell me you love me." He commanded me with his eyes, just the way he did when he was in charge.

"I love you..."

He groaned and rocked into me harder.

"Tell me you love me." My nails trailed down his neck to his back. I gripped the backs of his shoulders and dug deep.

"I love you, Tatum Titan." He kissed the corner of my mouth as he kept moving, kept grinding.

Hearing him say such a beautiful thing was the biggest turn-on. It aroused me more than whipping him. It satisfied me more than tying him to a chair and forbidding him from touching me. He gave me a new kind of high that I couldn't stop riding.

I moved with him as I lay underneath him, sharing hot kisses and sensual touches. My ankles pushed down on his ass, driving him deeper inside me. My moans grew louder, more uncontrollable. I panted and breathed, my nails cutting through his skin and sweat. I was about to come, and it was going to be an orgasm the likes of which I'd never had before.

My body tightened around him, and I gave his length a hard squeeze as I came. I flooded every inch of him with my overwhelming arousal, lubricating him so his thick cock could fit inside me even better, even deeper. "Diesel..." I came with a scream, pulling him farther into me. "Come with me."

He looked me in the eye as he kept thrusting. "No. I'd rather watch you—over and over."

I OPENED MY EYES THE NEXT MORNING AND LOOKED RIGHT into Hunt's face.

His eyes were heavy-lidded and barely open, but he wore that smile I'd fallen for. "Morning."

"Morning." It was the first time I hadn't set my alarm. His didn't go off either. I never took time off work, but right now, work didn't seem important. If there really was a catastrophe, Jessica knew she could call me.

"I like waking up to you."

"Me too..."

He pressed a kiss to my forehead and pulled my body closer to his. He hooked my legs over his waist, the way he preferred to cuddle with me. His strong muscles were warm like a furnace, and he heated the sheets with his natural body temperature. It would be perfect on a winter day. "How'd you sleep?"

"Good. You?"

"Really well. I finally don't feel tired."

"Really? Because we went to bed pretty late."

"Well, I slept like a rock. Making love to you can be exhausting...and exhilarating." He moved his hand into my hair and kissed the corner of my mouth. "Hungry? I've got some good stuff here, not just celery and water."

My eyes squinted at the insult. "When have you ever seen me eat celery?"

"With a Bloody Mary, I'm sure."

"I don't drink Bloody Marys."

"That's right...just pure whiskey."

"I'm a whiskey woman."

"No, you're my woman." He scooted out of bed then pulled on his sweatpants. "How about I make you breakfast in bed?"

"You don't need to do that. How about we make it together?"

He pulled one of his shirts out of a drawer and tossed it at me. "If you wear this."

"I'd love to." I pulled the cotton t-shirt over my head then followed him into the kitchen. We put on a pot of coffee, whipped up some eggs and veggies, and then sat down at the dining table.

Hunt ate shirtless. He was usually bare-chested around the house, which I preferred. He sipped his coffee and placed a few bites in his mouth. His gaze always found its way back to me. It felt like a regular day, but so much had changed overnight. Now everything was different. "When are you going to talk to Thorn?"

"I don't know. Maybe tomorrow."

"How do you think he'll take it?"

"He's already given me his blessing. Said I didn't owe him anything."

Hunt showed a small smile, the kind that reached his eyes. "That was big of him."

"He said a lot of sweet things, actually. Said if I didn't want to be with him, you were the next-best choice."

"Now I kinda feel bad for being such a dick to him."

"I wouldn't worry about it. Thorn doesn't hold grudges. He doesn't care about those sorts of things."

"Well, if he's gonna be an integral part of my life, I'll

have to spend time with him. Maybe we can go to a strip club or something..."

I smacked his arm playfully. "No strip club."

He chuckled. "You know you're the only woman I want to see strip."

"That's more like it."

His hand moved to mine on the table, and he held it. He kept enjoying his breakfast with a single hand, like showing this kind of affection was perfectly normal.

"Are you sure you really want to do this?"

He drank his coffee as he looked at me. "Why wouldn't I be sure?"

"You're committing to me for the rest of your life. It's a big deal."

"Doesn't scare me."

"How does it not?"

He took another drink of his coffee before he set it down. "When you told me about your arrangement with Thorn, I was judgmental about it. Told you I didn't like it. But the more I got to know you, the more I began to understand it. Why wouldn't Thorn want to have you as his wife? You're perfect."

"So not perfect, but whatever."

"So, why wouldn't I want that? Why wouldn't I want to have a partner like you? Being married to Tatum Titan would be one of my biggest accomplishments.

People would see you on my arm and wonder what I did to get you. You're successful, smart, and beautiful. I couldn't do any better. And the fact that I actually like you just makes it better. I'm never gonna find another woman like you. Even if our attraction and lust die someday, I know I'll still love you and respect you— forever." He squeezed my hand.

It wasn't the proposal that women fantasized about, but it was exactly what I wanted. I wanted a partner I could rely on, someone that I could trust. When time wore down our bodies and sucked away our beauty, there would still be loyalty and respect underneath. We would still take over the world—as partners. "If you're sure."

"I am sure. Are you?"

My fingers wrapped around my mug, feeling the heat from the ceramic material. "I think it's the best of both worlds. It's exactly what I want...and I can be married to someone I love as well. Thorn and I are very close, and he's a handsome man...but I've never felt that way about him. He's never felt that way about me."

"So how is this going to work?"

"You should be more specific."

"Transitioning from him to me."

"Thorn said we should break it off mutually so it doesn't hurt either one of us. And he said he wanted me to wait awhile before I start seeing you publicly. Could hurt me as well as him."

Hunt nodded. "True. How long?"

"Thorn and I were together for a long time...so at least six months."

Hunt whistled under his breath. "That's a long time...but reasonable. And how will our relationship work? Will that have rules?"

"You know me, Diesel. I love rules."

He squeezed my hand. "I do."

"I'd still like to be in charge sometimes...if you're open to that."

He grinned. "I'm open to that anytime. But the same goes for me, right?"

"Yes."

"Then perfect. Half and half. What about kids?"

"I'm getting old, from a pregnancy perspective. I need to have our first child by the time I'm thirty-two."

"Damn, then I'm gonna have to knock you up as soon as we're married."

"Yeah, probably."

"Sounds fine to me. You know I love giving you my come as it is."

"You want children, right?" I asked. "Because if you don't want children..."

"I do," he said quickly. "Honestly, I'm surprised you

do. That sounds like something you might not be interested in."

"I'm very interested. I don't have a family of my own, so I need to make one."

His eyes fell, his eyebrows furrowing. "That's not true. You have Thorn. You have me."

"I know...but someone of the same blood."

"Blood doesn't bind people any closer together than water." He grabbed his mug again and took a long drink.

It took me a moment to understand what that meant. Hunt didn't have a relationship with his father or his brother, and he probably never would. I squeezed his hand, our fingers intertwining together.

"How are the last names going to work?"

"I'm not changing my last name," I said firmly.

"Our kids are going by Hunt, not Titan."

I narrowed my eyes.

"At least compromise with a hyphen. Hunt-Titan."

"Titan-Hunt."

"Nope." He glared at me. "You're lucky I'm letting you have the hyphen at all."

"Lucky, huh?" I asked. "We can revisit the conversation later."

"Prenup?" he asked, changing the subject.

"Definitely."

He didn't make an argument against it, probably

knowing it was much simpler to protect our assets now. If we ever divorced, it would be a nightmare. "Okay. I think this worked out in Thorn's favor?"

"How so?"

"One day, he's gonna meet someone and fall hard. He'd regret being married."

"I don't know about that," I said. "Thorn isn't really the romantic type."

"I wasn't the romantic type either. I couldn't picture myself ever getting married. But then I met the right person...and all of that changed."

My eyes softened.

"And when he meets the right person, he'll be glad you met me."

I waited in line until I ordered my coffee. It was a beautiful day and I was in a good mood, so I wandered across the street from my building and decided to treat myself to a maple latte. People indulged in comfort food when they were sad, but I seemed to have the opposite problem.

Now that I was happy, I wanted the sweeter things.

I hadn't spoken to Thorn about it yet, but we were bound to cross paths today or tomorrow. And he probably had a suspicion this was going to be my answer anyway. I finally moved to the front of the line, ordered my coffee, and then stood off to the side as I waited. A few people stared at me, some even snapping pictures on their phones. I didn't consider myself to be famous, but anyone who worked in the business world knew exactly who I was.

"Titan." Brett appeared in front of me, wearing the same smile that Hunt possessed. With the same structured jawline and masculine features, it was surprising that I hadn't realized they were related the moment I was in the same room with them. "Midday coffee break, huh?"

"I need some gas. I'm running on empty."

"I know what you mean." He was in dark jeans and a black jacket, looking casual and cool.

"What are you doing here?"

"Just finished a meeting with a client. I've been working on the next model for the Bullet. I've been picking people's brains about it."

"Cool. I'm sure Diesel had an opinion or two."

Brett's eyes narrowed when I said his first name.

I tried to pretend that I did it on purpose and hadn't said anything I shouldn't. "Run it by me when you're finished. I might want an upgrade by the time you're done with it."

"Might have to just give you one. Having you be one of the sponsors of my cars has spiked sales like crazy."

"I'm glad the commercial worked so well."

"I saw the stuff you did with Connor Suede." He gave a thumbs-up. "Very classy. I loved it."

"Thanks."

"I might have to start wearing his clothes now."

"He can throw something spectacular together at the snap of a finger."

"Yeah, I believe it," he said. "I'm always hearing that guy is a genius."

"He is." I always paid respect where it was due, and Connor had earned it.

"So, you and Hunt talk regularly?"

"Yeah...we run a business together."

He nodded his head slowly, his expression hardening. "You know, Hunt is a pretty great guy. I know he's sarcastic and moody sometimes, but he's got a heart of gold underneath all those suits...and I know he really cares about you."

"Yeah...thanks." Now this conversation was getting awkward, like Brett was trying to tell me something without actually saying it.

"Thorn may be richer than him and come from a better family, but Hunt has just as much to offer."

What? What was that supposed to mean?

"Excuse me?"

"I'm just saying…"

"And why are you just saying this? Hunt and I are just business associates and friends."

His eyes narrowed, and he tried to hide his smile at the exact same time. It made his face change, looking contradictory and confusing. He straightened his jacket then broke eye contact. "Yeah…of course." He glanced at his watch. "I should get going, Titan. I'll see you around." He walked out without even giving me the chance to say goodbye.

I prided myself on my intuition, and I recognized that something was off. Brett was different from how he usually was, and the way he spoke about Hunt and me was simply suspicious. He wouldn't have said any of those things unless he thought Hunt and I were sleeping together.

Did that mean Hunt told him?

When he promised me he wouldn't?

I had to give Hunt the benefit of the doubt and assume he didn't. But that didn't mean I wasn't going to ask him about it.

I WAS ON MY WAY TO HUNT'S APARTMENT WHEN I CALLED

Thorn.

"Hey, what's up?" He picked up on the second ring, always taking my calls no matter what he was doing. He could be in the middle of a huge meeting but would still answer to see if I needed something.

"Nothing. You busy?" I sat in the back seat of the car while my driver took me to Hunt's penthouse.

"Never too busy for you. Have you thought more about your little love triangle problem?"

I rolled my eyes. "Not a love triangle."

"Kinda is," he said with a chuckle. "Have you made any decisions?"

Thorn already told me he was okay with breaking off the arrangement, but I still felt terrible for my final decision. We'd made plans for a lifetime together. Now I was walking away from all of that, from a reality where he would have been my husband. I had never been in love with Thorn, but I loved him deeply. "I talked to Hunt… and I want to be with him."

There was a long pause over the phone. A held breath. But when Thorn spoke a second later, everything seemed normal. "Well, I'm happy for you. He's a good guy, so I know you're in good hands."

"He said he wants to offer me what you offered…so he wants to get married and have a partnership. We just also happen to be in love."

"Wow. That's exactly what you wanted."

"Yeah…"

"Well, I'm a little disappointed he stole my genius idea, but I'm still happy for you."

"Really?" I asked, needing his approval more than anything else.

"Of course, Titan. Don't even think twice about it."

The car pulled up to the curb, and I walked into the lobby. "I'm glad you're okay with this."

"We're still a team. You'll still be my number one girl."

I stepped into the elevator and watched the doors close. "That's true."

"And maybe I'll ask Hunt to go golfing or something."

"He said he was going to ask you to a strip club."

"Hell yeah," he said with a laugh. "Now that's more like it."

The elevator rose to the top then opened into his living room. I stepped inside, seeing Hunt sitting on the couch in just his sweatpants. "Well, I've gotta go. I'll talk to you later."

"Alright, Titan. See you around." He hung up.

Hunt set aside the book he was reading and walked over to me. His arms moved around my waist, and he smiled down at me. "Who was that?"

"Judging by that smile, you know exactly who it was."

"Thorn?"

"Yeah."

"And did you tell him?"

I nodded.

His grin widened. "So you're officially mine, huh?"

"Officially. Just not according to the media."

"Well, that'll change eventually." He rubbed his nose against mine, looking at me with affection in his eyes. "He took it well, then?"

"Of course he did."

"Great."

"He said you guys should go golfing together."

"He didn't like my strip club idea?"

"Actually, he liked it a little too much."

He chuckled. "Maybe he and I have more in common than I realized." He kissed the corner of my mouth before he guided me to the couch. "How was your day?"

I thought of my coffee encounter with Brett. "Something interesting happened today, actually."

"Yeah." He sat down and rested his arm over my shoulders. Even when he was sitting, his abs were smooth and tight.

"I ran into Brett." I watched every little reaction he

made, studying him like he was a competitor sitting across from me in a conference room.

"Yeah? What did he say?"

"Some stuff about work...and then he said some weird stuff about us."

Hunt's expression didn't change at all.

"Saying you were a good guy...and you just as much to offer as Thorn."

Still, nothing.

The lack of reaction was even more suspicious to me. "Diesel...did you tell him?"

"Tell him what?"

"About us."

Hunt held my gaze, his jaw slowly tightening. His eyes began to fill with frustration, a look of annoyance he couldn't hide.

I knew he wouldn't lie to me, so I waited for the truth.

He dropped his arms from my shoulders and released a sigh. "Yes...I did."

Betrayal immediately flooded through me once the truth was out. I'd asked him not to say anything, but he did it anyway. He even told him about Thorn. "Diesel—"

"Let me explain before you get mad."

My mouth was still open, but the words stopped coming.

"He accused me of it. He kept asking questions about us, kept saying I look at you in a different way. And then it just kept going and going...until there was no point in hiding it. He knew. Whether I admitted it or not, he knew. So I thought it was best if I came clean about it and asked him not to mention it."

"And then he mentions it to me?" I asked incredulously. "Imagine who else he's told."

"I promise you he hasn't told anyone."

"Sure didn't have a problem spilling the beans to me."

"Because you're involved. He's just protective of me... looking out for me."

"Did you tell him about our arrangement?" Smoke was practically coming out of my ears because I was so pissed.

"No. He thinks you and Thorn just have an open relationship."

I moved away from Hunt because I needed to pace in his living room, to have some space.

Hunt leaned forward and watched me. "I'm sorry, baby. But he figured it out. This is why I wanted to tell my friends about it. That way I could just tell them to keep quiet about it."

"Looks like Brett has a big mouth to me."

"I promise he won't say anything to anyone. You have my word, alright?"

I dragged my hands down my face and groaned.

"Look, he's known about it for a while now. If he was going to tell someone, you would know by now. So obviously, he hasn't."

"Why did he tell me you're a good guy and just as good as Thorn?"

"Because...I told him that I was falling for you, and I wanted to be with you. I didn't know what to do. So he told me to fight for you, that women like you don't grow on trees. That's all."

It was so sweet that I couldn't be mad.

"He's to me what Thorn is to you. You can trust him."

I'd always liked Brett. He treated me with respect and always made me feel welcome. He had a charming smile, a comforting presence. I knew he and Hunt were a lot alike, that they shared the same philosophy on life and loyalty. Hunt turned his back on his family to support Brett. Brett wouldn't betray him after doing that.

Hunt stood up and faced me, keeping a few feet in between us. "Baby?"

I sighed.

"Come on."

"What?"

"Don't be mad at me."

I ran my fingers through my hair, forcing myself to cool off.

"Alright?"

"Okay…I'm not mad. Just annoyed."

"Well, I'm sorry about that."

I crossed my arms over my chest, knowing I couldn't stay angry with Hunt. If Brett figured it out on his own, what was Hunt supposed to do? Lie to his only family in the world?

Hunt stepped closer to me, his hands moving to my hips. He pressed his forehead to mine and looked down at my lips. "Are we okay?"

I nodded.

"You know I would never betray you on purpose."

"I know, Diesel."

"And now that we're moving forward with this, I'm gonna have to tell my friends. It's been nearly impossible keeping it a secret this long."

"Okay. Just don't tell anyone about Jeremy…"

"I never would." He grabbed my chin and lifted my gaze to meet his expression. "You know that. I would never betray any of your secrets. I just want the world to know we're together. That's all I care about. Whatever story you want to tell, it doesn't matter to me. But at the end of the day…I want the world to know you're mine."

11

HUNT

Brett entered my office, smiling like he was on top of the world. "Miss me already?"

I asked him to swing by while he was in town. He usually moved around a lot, going wherever the automobile business took him. "I never miss you."

"Doesn't seem like it." He took a seat and crossed his legs, looking smug for sitting in someone else's office.

"Thanks for blowing everything to Titan." I knew my brother had the best intentions, but I didn't appreciate him running his mouth like a goddamn idiot. Luckily, she wasn't angry with me. If this had been a few weeks ago, things could have turned out quite differently. Fortunately, the woman already knew I loved her.

"What?"

"Don't play stupid with me. She told me about your coffee visit."

"I didn't say anything."

"No, but the woman is a genius. She can read between the lines pretty well. Titan is a mastermind. You better not forget that."

His smile faded away when he realized I was seriously upset. "I didn't mean anything by it. I just don't like how she's dragging you along."

"She's not dragging me along."

"Seems that way."

"Actually, she and I talked, and she said she wants to be with me."

Brett's smile returned, but this time, it wasn't smug. It was genuine, the kind that reached his eyes. "Really? So she's leaving Thorn?"

"Yeah."

"Good. So you finally got off your ass and fought for her."

"Something like that," I said quietly.

"So Tatum Titan is officially your girlfriend."

"Well, not officially. You still can't tell anyone until Titan is ready."

He rolled his eyes. "Why is everything a secret with you guys?"

"Because that's how she wants it. So, can I trust you to shut up?"

He rolled his eyes again. "I would never throw you under the bus. You know that."

I did.

"So, can I act like I know now? When I see Titan?"

"Yes. But make sure she understands you aren't going to blab to everyone."

"Alright, I will." Brett rested his chin on his fingertips as he stared at me.

"What?"

"You're happy. It's a nice change."

I was happy. Instead of being dark and brooding all the time, I had something to smile about. Not only had I finally fallen in love with someone, but I'd found the perfect woman. I found someone I adored, someone I respected, someone I truly enjoyed. I'd always thought if I ever settled down, my wife would be a housewife, spending my money and lavishing herself with gifts. She would have a nanny watch the kids so she could go to yoga. Basically, a trophy wife. But instead, I was getting the most badass woman on the planet.

Tatum Titan.

She was the kind of woman who would truly make me into a man.

"Yeah...I am happy."

Brett winked. "That's all I wanted."

"Sir, Thorn Cutler is here to see you."

This should be good. "Send him in. Thank you, Natalie." I left my seat and moved around my desk so I could greet him properly. Any other time we interacted with each other, we always intimidated each other with our desks and offices.

But that was behind us now.

Thorn stepped inside, looking like a real executive in his black suit. His blue eyes and dirty-blond hair made him look more like a model than a business owner. I wasn't threatened by anyone, but I was grateful Titan had never been interested in him. He had just as much to offer—and he'd risked his life to save hers.

He wore a slight smile and extended his hand.

I took it and shook it firmly. "Nice to see you, Thorn." I spoke genuinely, truly making an effort to put everything in the past.

"You too." He moved his hands into his pockets, wearing a slight smile. "I came by to congratulate you... and hit you up on that strip club."

I chuckled. "My lady wouldn't go for that. But I'm always up for a round of golf."

"Are you any good?"

I shrugged. "Pretty good, actually."

"Then we'll have to hit the links together. That's where I have most of my meetings anyway."

"Anytime."

"For now, you wanna get a drink?"

It was noon, but Thorn and Titan obviously started drinking as early as nine. I'd have to fit in. "Always."

WE WENT TO A SPORTS BAR A FEW BLOCKS AWAY. WE SAT in a booth together, and if anyone recognized us, they would probably assume we were just doing business.

Thorn had a beer, and I ordered the same thing. Titan would be drinking an Old Fashioned by now, but I wasn't quite there. A beer was good for now.

"So," Thorn said. "I guess we're friends now?"

"I'd like to be friends. I know it would mean a lot to Titan."

"You're right, it would. I know I've always given you a hard time, but I've always respected you, Hunt."

"I know. And the feeling is mutual."

He clanked his beer against mine. "I'll drink to that."

I took a long drink before returning the glass to the coaster.

"Just take care of her, alright? She's a tough cookie,

but she has needs. She hides them from everyone, but they're there if you look hard enough."

"I've picked up on that."

"And don't drag her name through the mud. If you ever do anything to cross her, I'll have to declare you as my mortal enemy. I want the two of us to get along, and I'm sure we will, but I have to put that out there."

"I understand, Thorn."

He drank his beer and looked at the TV in the corner. "I knew you were different. The second you came around, I thought I might lose her. All the other guys...they just came and went. But every time I saw the way she looked at you, I knew you were going to be a problem."

"Thanks for letting her go. I imagine that was hard."

He shrugged. "She was the perfect partner. I'd love to grow old with her. But you know what? We still will grow old together. No matter who she loves, we'll still be close friends. And if she has a chance to fall in love again and be happy, good for her. I'd never stand in the way of that."

"Thanks."

"And I can tell you love her too. She really set you straight."

"Yeah, she did." Now that Thorn and I were no longer competitors, it was easy to talk to him. He was easygoing, transparent, friendly. I could see him being a part of my crew eventually. "Now, when you meet the right person, you'll be unencumbered."

"Unencumbered?" he asked with a grin. "I'm not really a one-woman kind of guy. I'm sure Titan told you that."

"I thought the same thing about myself...until she walked into my life."

"Well, I've known Titan for a long time. She's wicked smart, beautiful, funny...the perfect woman. But you know what I felt for her?" He shook his head. "Nothing. And if I can't fall in love with my favorite person in the world, then it's not in the cards for me. I don't think there's anything wrong with that. That's just how I am."

I still believed all of that would change if the right woman crossed his path. Maybe Titan was the perfect woman for me, but she wasn't the right partner for him. "Never say never..."

He chuckled like the subject was funny. "I'm sure Titan told you I'm the controller just the way she is."

"The controller?"

"Yes. The person in charge. I like to run my women the same way I run a business. I'm far too controlling to have a spontaneous and real relationship. But I'm okay with that. And the women I meet along the way are okay with it too."

"You were the one who introduced her to the lifestyle?"

"Yeah. She had a lot of issues after I killed Jeremy. Mainly trust issues. I told her you didn't need trust if you were always in control. Your partner had to give the trust, but you weren't required to do the same in return. That worked really well for her."

"Until me."

He nodded. "Yep. Now that she's happy, she can trust again. It's great."

"It is great."

He pulled up his sleeve to look at his watch. "I should probably get back to work. How about golf on Tuesday?"

"Sure. Have your assistant call mine."

"Will do." Instead of shaking my hand, he fist-bumped me.

The corner of my mouth rose in a smile. "Is this how you say goodbye to your friends?"

"No. You?"

"No."

He shrugged then got out of the booth. "Then let's pretend that shit never happened."

12

TITAN

I was sitting at my desk when my phone lit up with a text message.

Your panties are sitting in my pocket.

I cocked an eyebrow when I looked at the message from Hunt. But, of course, I smiled too. *How did they wind up there?*

I took them.

Perv.

Only for you.

He stopped texting me, and I went back to work, doing my best to not think about the man waiting for me as soon as the day was over. Now that my life had changed so much, it was hard to remember how it used to be. Arrangements seemed like a thing of the past. I didn't need rules to have good sex, to feel safe with my partner.

Hunt made me feel safe on his own.

An hour went by, and I finished a phone call with one of my suppliers in China. I filtered through a few emails, trying to multitask and get as much done as possible. My assistants couldn't do everything since I was the one who had to make all the final decisions.

My phone rang, and Thorn's name appeared on the screen.

I took it without stopping my email. "Hey, what's up? Hunt told me he had fun with you yesterday."

Angry silence.

I picked up on all of Thorn's moods because I knew them better than anyone. "What's wrong?"

He sighed.

This was bad. He usually spat out his thoughts by now. "Thorn...what is it?"

"I don't know how to say this. It's bad, Titan. Fucking bad."

My hands pulled away from the keyboard, and I turned into the phone. Everything on my checklist faded to the background when I heard the bitterness in his voice. He was so angry, he wasn't even yelling.

And that was the deepest level of anger. "What?"

He sighed again before he spoke. "Google yourself."

"What...?"

"There's an article about you in the *Times*. Hunt told them about Jeremy."

Now I was the one who turned silent, thinking so many things that I couldn't form words. My breathing picked up, and I could hear it echo back at me. When the phone rang on my landline, I immediately yanked the wire out. If this was article was true, I was about to be bombarded with reporters.

"Titan?" Thorn's angry voice came through the phone. "Say something."

I couldn't say anything.

"The article just appeared five minutes ago. Give it thirty minutes, and the whole world is going to know about it."

God, I couldn't believe this was happening.

I moved to my computer, typed in my name, and right at the top, the article appeared. The headline alone made me want to hurl.

Tatum Titan: Victim of Domestic Abuse.

No. No. No.

The article was long, and that didn't bode well either.

"Titan?" Thorn repeated.

"I..." I couldn't think of anything better to say. "Fuck."

"There's no mention of Jeremy's death being suspicious. But that could change if people keep digging."

"This can't be happening..."

"I'm gonna kill Hunt. That fucking prick sat across from me yesterday like everything was fine. He'd probably already talked to the reporter by then." He screamed into the phone, something crashing off his desk and hitting the floor.

"What makes you so certain it was Hunt?" Right now, anyone was a suspect. But Hunt wasn't the first person who came to mind. Only Thorn and I knew about the incident with Jeremy. Hunt was the first person we told. But still...I couldn't believe he would do that to me.

"The reporter named him as the source."

My heart sank. It plummeted into my stomach. When it reached the floor of my belly, it exploded into dozens of pieces. I was nauseated, sick, and weak. I didn't even feel rage because I was so stunned. Betrayal had never hurt this much, had never stabbed me so deeply. There was a knife in my back, and it kept turning and twisting even though I was already dead. "My god..."

"Fucking asshole. I can't believe he would fuck with us like this."

"Why did he do this...?"

"I don't fucking know. Maybe to hurt both of us. We're contenders on the *Forbes* list."

"But Hunt isn't psycho like that."

"Obviously, he is. You don't know him...I don't know him."

My hand was shaking as I held the phone to my ear. Now that all the evidence was stacked against Hunt, there was nothing I could do but accept the painful truth. He was the only person I told about Jeremy, and the reporter mentioned him by name.

He did this.

He did this on purpose.

"I have to go..."

"What are you doing?" Thorn asked. "Do you want me to come to you?"

"No. I'm going to Hunt's office. I'm giving that son of a bitch a piece of my mind."

13

HUNT

I WAS SITTING at my desk, Titan's panties in my pocket, when the door flew open and Titan stormed inside.

Natalie was trailing behind her. "Sir, I tried to—"

"Get the fuck out." Titan pointed to the doorway, enraged in a tight black skirt with a black blouse. She didn't look like the powerful executive I was used to seeing from eight to five. Now she looked maniacal, like she was going to set my office on fire and burn down the building.

Natalie shrank against the wall then darted out of the room, knowing Titan wasn't an opponent she could face. Her job wasn't worth the feud.

Titan slammed the door so hard it seemed like she shook the building.

Or it was just in my imagination.

I got out of my chair and stood upright, my body

immediately sensing a battle about to take place. I didn't have a clue what would provoke Titan to be this unprofessional and storm into my office like this.

But whatever it was, it was bad.

"Baby, what's wrong?"

"Don't you fucking dare." She stormed to my desk, her heels not breaking their stride as she marched right up to me. She pulled her hand back and slapped me so hard across the face I actually stumbled back. "I trusted you. I fucking trusted you."

My skin immediately smarted from the momentum, turning bright red from the attack. I turned back to her, pissed that she'd slapped me in my own office like she owned the place. "What the fuck are you—"

She slapped me again.

Now I lost my temper. I charged her and grabbed her by the elbow. "Hit me again, and see what happens." I flung her arm down, looking into a face as furious as mine.

She steadied her hand this time, but murder was still in her eyes. "Don't play stupid with me. You probably already read the article—twice."

"Article?"

"You want me to hit you again?" she threatened. "Then straighten up and be honest. Don't insult me by playing stupid with me."

"I seriously have no idea what you're talking about."

She shook her head, her eyes narrowed. "The *New York Times* quoted you as their source in the article, and you're still are going to play stupid with me? How much of an idiot do you think I am?"

New York Times? I was their source? What the hell was going on? "I didn't go to the *New York Times* and say anything about you—"

"You're the only person who knows other than Thorn. So it had to have been you. Stop the games. Just admit that you got me. You played me. You tricked me, got me into bed, stole my secrets, and then turned around and sold them." She threw her arms up. "So congratulations, Hunt. You taught me a lesson that I already learned once."

My mind worked furiously to catch up to what she was saying. "About Jeremy?" I headed back to my desk and quickly typed the subject into the search bar. An instant later, the article popped up. I saw the headline and immediately turned white.

"Stop with the act!"

"Tatum, I really—"

She marched to my desk with her finger pointed at me. "Don't call me that."

I turned back to the computer and skimmed the article. No wonder why she was pissed. And lo and behold, the reporter named me as his primary source. What the fuck was going on? "Titan, I swear to you I had nothing to do with this."

"Fuck you. Don't insult me."

"Titan, look at me." I placed my hand over my heart. "I know this looks really bad, but I swear to you I didn't do any of this. I'm being framed."

"By who?" she asked incredulously. "Thorn? Because he's the only person who knows."

"I...I don't know. But by somebody because I would never do this to you. I wouldn't do this to anybody."

"Cut the shit, Hunt."

I came around the desk and got in her face. "You know me, Titan. I would never betray you like this. Come on, think about it. I know I look really bad right now, and I can't blame you for jumping to conclusions, but I honestly didn't do it."

She crossed her arms over her chest, staring at me like I was utter scum.

"What would I get out of this, Titan? You're my business partner. Why would I want to make you look bad?"

"No idea. But I don't care."

I was losing her. "Titan, just think for a second. You know me. You know me better than anyone—"

"I thought I did. But you're an asshole like all the rest." She marched to the door, officially done with me.

"Whoa, hold on." I grabbed her by the elbow and steadied her.

She twisted out of my grasp quicker than a viper. "Don't ever touch me again."

I held my hands up and didn't touch her again. "Just let me get the reporter on the phone. I'll get to the bottom of this, alright?"

She only stared at me, but that was better than nothing. She could just leave, and I wouldn't be able to stop her. She tightened her arms over her chest, her look still furious but a little less potent.

I pressed my palms together in a gesture of gratitude. "Thank you." I walked out of my office to where my four assistants sat, and they were all whispering about what had just happened with Titan. "I need to get the reporter from the *New York Times* on the phone."

"Which reporter?" Natalie asked.

"The stupid bitchface that wrote the article."

Natalie flinched at my rage. "I...I don't know what article you're talking about."

"Goddammit." I moved to her computer and leaned over her, typing in the article and finding his name. "Just get this guy on the phone...Jared Newman. Now." I walked back into the office, hoping Titan had calmed down a little more.

But she didn't.

The bottom drawer in my desk was open, and she held the folder in her hands. With smoldering eyes that could kill, she stared me down. They were full of moisture, but not because she was about to shed tears of heartbreak. They were furious, maniacal tears. They were the kind of tears that could only be created through sheer frustration. She tossed the folder across the room, papers flying everywhere.

Fuck.

She marched toward me, her arms tensed by her sides. She didn't look like she was going to hit me this time. The look she gave me was worse. It was an expression of pure loathing, of abundant hatred. She didn't want to slap me because her palm was too good for my face.

"Titan..." I breathed through the pain in my chest, knowing how bad this looked. "I got that folder a long time ago, but I swear I never read it—"

"I don't care, Hunt." She pressed her face close to mine as she whispered. She wasn't screaming anymore, throwing papers around the room and causing a scene. Now she was quiet and calculating, her eyes glossy as more moisture flooded her gaze. The vein in her forehead was throbbing, and her eyes were about to pop out of her head. Her jaw was tenser than mine had ever been. "I got mine, Hunt. But trust me...you'll get yours."

ALSO BY VICTORIA QUINN

The story continues in Boss Woman

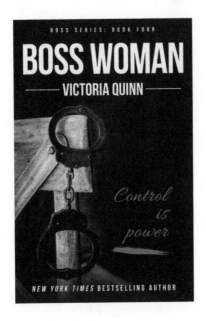

Order Now

CPSIA information can be obtained
at www.ICGtesting.com
Printed in the USA
LVHW02s0044280818
588281LV00001B/196/P

9 781979 158558